Kimba's Christmas

Kimba's Christmas

by
Meg Welch Dendler

SERENITY MOUNTAIN PUBLISHING
Springdale, Arkansas

Published by Serenity Mountain Publishing

Kimba's Christmas

©2019 by Meg Welch Dendler. All rights reserved.

Printed in the United States of America.

www.megdendler.com

ISBN 978-1733645065

Cover design by Kelsey Rice.

Photos by Scott and Meg Dendler.

The characters and events in this book

are not based on real events.

Well, maybe a little bit.

But the names have been changed

to protect the innocent.

Sometimes.

All of the stories in this series are full of real events in the lives of our cats Kimba and Hiro. You will find photos of them at the end of many chapters, as well as photos of other cats and events that sparked my imagination.

Of course, Kimba and Hiro don't really talk to alien cats in our bathroom mirror, nor do they visit ships in space. Not that I've ever seen. Maybe they are just tricky.

You never know with cats.

*Some cats are born on Earth and
never know who they really are.
Others are sent.
They are undercover
for their years on Earth.
They know who they are.
They know that they are not
from Earth at all.
And they are part of a bigger plan.*

TABLE OF CONTENTS

So Far In The Series:

S tarting with Book Five in any series is a bad idea. Go back and read the first four books if you really want to enjoy this one. For those of you determined to start here, or in case you read the first books a while ago and need a reminder, here are some details you should know.

1) All cats (wild and tame) are aliens from a planet that is so far away they live on spaceships all over the universe instead of going back. They have plans for a complete takeover of Earth—when the time is right.

2) Most of the cats on Earth do not know where they came from anymore. The old stories have been lost. They don't know they are aliens and are quite happy being pets. Some are just wild or lost or stray.

3) Specially trained agent cats from the ships spend time on Earth. They pretend to be regular cats, but they are not.

4) Agent cats communicate with the ship and each other through reflective devices. Mirrors are the best and most common ways to communicate.

5) Ship cats live for hundreds of Earth years. An Earth-life is just a fraction of that. When an agent dies on Earth, their being is transferred back to the ship. Agents rarely return to Earth more than nine times.

6) The two main characters in this series, Kimba and Hiro, are sisters and littermates who were accidentally born on Earth. A human (Daddy) found them and took them in before they could return to the ship. Their mother is the high commander of all the cat ships in the known universes. It is their destiny to follow in her paw prints as the highest-ranking cats.

7) Once Kimba and Hiro learned who they really are, they started training for their future as alien cat leaders. They travel back and forth between their Earth home and the cat spaceship headquarters.

8) Special Agent Artemis is the main contact on the ship. He watches over the two royal daughters and ensures their safety on Earth.

9) Kimba has completed her training and is now officially an agent. Hiro is not that interested in her ship life. She loves her human Daddy too much. She just hopes to be on the High Council one day.

10) Miss Fatty Cat (aka Agent Ebony) lives in the house with Kimba and Hiro. She belongs to the younger daughter in the family, Leia. Miss Fatty Cat is rather lazy and loves Leia's attention.

11) Slinky (aka Agent Onyx) is the younger sister of Miss Fatty Cat. She lives in an apartment with the older daughter in the family, Mindy. A dog named Dottie (aka The Wiggly Black Beast) has come to live with them.

12) Life on the ships is highly organized. All kittens follow in their parents' profession in an orderly system that has continued for millions of years. Long-term contact with the democratic process on Earth has stirred up resistance to this system. A group of rebels, the League For Cat Equality, is

fighting the established system. Commander Horus is in charge.

13) Miss Fatty Cat sneakily helped the rebels kidnap Kimba in order to force the high commander to listen to their new ideas, but no proof of her help could be found. Miss Fatty Cat had her own motives and jealousies, but she came to regret being involved at all.

14) Kimba was saved from her kidnappers by Transfer Technician in Training Thoth and her uncle, Special Agent Buddy. Another transfer technician named Snowball was captured and blamed for the plot against Kimba.

15) When Slinky was accidentally locked out of her apartment and became lost, a team, including Thoth and Kimba, helped find and rescue her. Through this adventure, Kimba realized Thoth would make an excellent agent and convinced her parents to break all of the traditions on the ship and allow him into agent training. Thoth is now an agent, despite the fact that there has never been an agent in his family in all of known history.

16) Kimba and Hiro have now settled into their Earth-lives and routine and are enjoying being well-loved pets, but they know the time will come when High Commander Felicity, their mother, will call them back to the ship permanently.

O CHRISTMAS TREE

Kimba watched in fascination as prickery green plastic branches of different lengths and a tall metal stick came together to form an indoor tree. Her humans came up with the strangest ideas.

It was that fabulous time of year again. For a few weeks, Christmas changed everything.

Each year, assembling this tree in the house happened right after Thanksgiving and the big turkey party. It was part of her family's holiday traditions.

As a kitten, Kimba had learned that climbing the giant fake tree would send the humans into a panic. It was a temptation and a challenge that had been hard to resist. She would hide underneath, and when no one was watching, she could leap up inside the branches lickety-split. If she stayed still, she could hide there for hours. But with all the dangling, sparkling ornaments, being still was impossible. She'd stretch her paw out to snag one, and the game would be over.

The girls would squeal, "Kimba's in the tree again!" And Mama would yell, "No! No!" Daddy would reach in with his big hands, pull the white kitten out, and plop her on the floor.

Now that she was more grown up, Kimba didn't bother climbing into the tree anymore. It was plastic, so she couldn't dig in her claws or really enjoy the experience. But she did love to lie underneath it and watch the sparkling lights. As Daddy set up the tree, Kimba knew she would be napping underneath it shortly.

The humans often shared stories of their Christmas trees over the years, and Kimba had learned that sometimes a real tree was part of the tradition, instead of the plastic put-together one. The family had gone to a shop and bought a fresh tree. It had then been carefully set up in the living room and supplied with fresh water. More than once, even though the pine tree had been cut down from its roots, it had started to grow new shoots off the ends of the branches.

Daddy found that fascinating and often suggested they get a real tree next year. Then Mama would remind him of the time that water from the base of a real tree had ruined the wood floors in the living room. From what Kimba could put together, that was one of the last years a real tree came into the house.

A real tree with bark that she could dig her claws into sounded much more interesting than the cold, hard plastic pole at the center of the fake tree. If Daddy ever got a real tree again, Kimba was certain she would try to climb it. She'd never climbed a real tree before, but she imagined it would be thrilling. Her claws flexed in and out at the thought of it.

Once the assembly of the different layers of branches was done, Daddy wrapped strands of lights up and down and around the tree. Mama followed with shiny gold garland. Then Leia carefully placed ornaments all over the tree, talking about why each was special and when they had found it.

"Spider-Man goes at the top," Daddy said when Leia tried to hang that ornament too low.

"I have Rudolph here," Mama said, "but who has the Bumble? They should all be together."

Kimba's heart raced watching those magical, dangling toys sparkle from the branches. The soft ones Mama placed on the lowest branches had tiny bells attached.

"These should distract them," Mama said, "in case the kitties forget the rules."

Kimba lashed her tail, knowing she would capture one of two of those soft ornaments before morning.

In her eight years with her much-loved Earth family, Kimba had witnessed this routine over and over. Boxes were brought down from the attic above the carport, and piles of odd-smelling items were stacked all over the living room. It was the same routine here in the new mountaintop house in Arkansas as it had been back in Houston when she was just a kitten.

The cat Nativity was displayed on the mantle over the fireplace, and the stockings were hung with care. There was one for each human and one for each cat. There was even one for The Big Black Beast.

Kimba had a special pink stocking with a white cat wearing a glittery crown on the front. She blinked happily at the sight of it. Before the Christmas celebrations were done, Mama would tuck some special treats into that stocking.

Daddy laid a white mat under the tree and set up all the little ceramic buildings and figures that went together to form his Christmas village. The elaborate process of shifting each house and little figure into just the perfect position went on for over an hour. Daddy was very particular about the final product, though he was sure to leave space for the cats to sleep under the tree as well and spots within the village for Hiro to sit. Hiro thought sitting in the village was a very important part of the holiday. Kimba preferred the challenge of tiptoeing through it without knocking a single figure down.

Out of the final set of boxes, Mama selected trinkets the girls had created over the years and all kinds of candles and statues, placing them around the living room. Finally, Mama stopped and put her hands on her hips, surveying the decorations.

"I think that's it," she declared.

Daddy returned the empty tubs and boxes to the attic, and Leia headed for her bedroom. But Kimba stayed in her spot on the sofa, enjoying the glow of the holiday lights.

Now that the commotion was over, Hiro wandered out of the bedroom to join her sister. She curled up a few feet away, watching the flickering lights of what Mama called the "disco ball" tree topper. Yellow and green and red splotches danced across the walls and the ceiling. Every year, just the same.

Miss Fatty Cat staggered out from Leia's bedroom, sniffing the air to take in all the new smells. She flumped up on the sofa near the sisters, and they all exchanged slow, content gazes.

"It's Christmas time again," Miss Fatty Cat said.

"Yep," Kimba murmured. "Everyone will be busy and happy, and there will be presents for everyone."

"Yep," Hiro said, curling up into a tighter ball and shutting her eyes.

Kimba's eyes drooped too, feeling the comfort and peace that always came with vacation and the family all celebrating together. Christmas was a most wonderful time of the year.

But all three cats stirred and their eyes grew wide as Daddy walked past again. He had returned from the attic with a giant going-away bag in each hand.

"What is he doing with those things?" Hiro asked in horror.

"Maybe we shouldn't have put up the tree this year," Mama said as Daddy dragged the suitcases past her. "What if the cats go wild and break things while we are gone?"

7

Daddy paused at the bedroom, set down the bags, looked at the cats, and then back at the tree.

"No," he said. "It's fine. They are big girls now and won't mess with it. And it would be weird to spend December with no tree in the house." He picked the suitcases back up. "I'm going to put these in our closet until the trip. I didn't want to have to go back up in the attic."

"Good idea," Mama said as she took one last look at the tree and then wandered into the kitchen.

Kimba looked at Hiro, who was frozen in fear. Hiro hated it when the family went away. Any day she didn't get kisses and cuddles from Daddy was sad and lonely for her, no matter how many other cats or people were around.

"I wonder when they are leaving," Kimba said. "It must not be right away if they are putting the bags in the closet."

Hiro didn't answer, but she curled her tail tightly around her body and tucked her nose into her front paws. Maybe if she didn't see them, the bags wouldn't be real and Daddy wouldn't actually go away.

8

Kimba looked up at the sparkling tree again and wondered, *What will Christmas be like without the family to help us celebrate?*

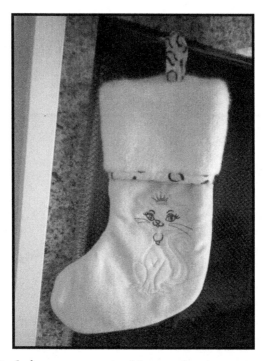

Kimba's very own stocking and an ornament
made from her paw print. Both are very pink.

2

KIMBA PLANS A TRIP

Music twinkled through the house as Mama cleaned the kitchen a few weeks later.

Jingle bells, jingle bells,
Jingle all the way.

Kimba kept Mama company, sitting on the kitchen window ledge and watching the bright-red birds jockey for seeds at the feeder in the yard. There was no snow that December, but it didn't matter to Kimba either way since she never went outside. It was chilly enough that Daddy would pile wood in the big black stove in the corner of the living room, and the cats would all find toasty spots to sleep in front of it. Winter fires and cuddly blankets made the season nothing but wonderful for Kimba, Hiro, and Miss Fatty Cat.

Mama finished her work and then scratched Kimba on the top of her white furry head.

Ah, the perfect spot. Kimba purred and closed her eyes.

"Time to go get some shopping done before the trip," Mama said.

The trip? Kimba had forgotten about the going-away bags and the possible absence of her humans. She hadn't heard anything more about it since they put the tree together.

Kimba watched as Mama and Daddy bundled into coats. As usual, Mama tried to get Leia to wear a heavy coat, but the teenager fussed and refused.

"Mom, I'm fine," she protested as she wiggled away from Mama's attempts to fasten her light jacket closed.

Mama put her hands on her hips, sighed, and picked up her purse to leave.

"Be good while we are gone, kitties," she called behind her as they went out the door. "Max, you are in charge!"

As always, The Big Black Beast wagged his tail eagerly. He loved being in charge.

With happy smiles, the three humans bustled out into the carport, talking about what gifts they needed to find for Mindy and Grandma.

Kimba didn't move from her spot on the counter until she saw the car turn off onto the highway at the end of the long country driveway. Then she hopped down and trotted to the master bedroom. Mama and Daddy's bathroom mirror was the main location for any communications with the ship. It was tucked away nicely and made it easy to hear if a human was coming. It was vital they never caught Kimba talking to a Cat in the Mirror.

Hiro was asleep on the big pillow on the cedar chest, where she spent most of her life, but Kimba didn't need her help to contact the ship. Her sister had never really had any interest in that. Hiro would be more than happy to spend every one of her possible Earth-lives on the planet with Daddy.

Jumping up onto the bathroom counter, Kimba settled herself properly and curled her tail around her front feet.

"Greetings," she said to her reflection in the glass.

That was the signal to let the Cat in the Mirror know the coast was clear. In a few seconds, Kimba's image blurred and the face of her friend Thoth appeared.

"Greetings," he said.

"Ah, good. I was hoping you would be on duty," Kimba said.

"Any contact from you always goes directly to me. The high commander wants to be sure nothing is left out or miscommunicated."

High Commander Felicity had personally set up a system for no one but Agent Thoth to accept messages from her youngest daughter. Thoth had saved Kimba's life twice, dangerously risking his own safety the second time in order to save her from an angry beast during a mission on Earth. The high commander knew he would do it again too, without a second thought. Anything Kimba-related went directly to Thoth, and Thoth thought this was a perfect arrangement.

"The humans have gone Christmas shopping," Kimba said. "It seemed like a good time to alert you to some developments here."

"What kind of developments?" Thoth asked, his hackles rising in worry. "Is there any danger? Should we bring you to the ship immediately?"

"Nothing like that. Everything is fine. The family will be taking a trip. I'm not sure exactly when. They got down the going-away bags a few weeks ago, but today Mama mentioned doing the shopping before the trip—like it would happen soon. Christmas is coming, and I hope they are not gone then. But I don't know yet."

"That is very standard human conduct. Families often take trips at the holidays. It is the busiest travel season of the year on the North American continent and a couple of others as well."

"What I'm wondering is if Mother would like me to come to the ship for more training during the vacation, like I did when they went to Florida a few Earth-years ago."

15

"That is certainly a possibility," he said as professionally as possible. His heart felt like it might leap out his chest.

"Daddy, the human male, brought the *huge* going-away bags down from the attic, so it must be a trip lasting several days at least. Definitely longer than a weekend. I will see what I can find out about dates and watch for when they start packing."

"I will inform the high commander," Thoth said. "She can begin to make plans for what special training and ship tours can be done during that time."

"I haven't been in the predator training rooms yet," Kimba said.

Her pupils widened and darkened with excitement at the thought of it. Thoth had told her stories about his training sessions in those rooms— climbing trees and escaping from skunks and badgers and even dangerous creatures like bears and coyotes. It was a part of agent training that Kimba had skipped, and that bothered her.

"Running for your life from an angry beast in a tiny Earth apartment wasn't enough?" he asked.

Knowing she had been in that much danger had certainly been enough for him. His tail puffed and his whiskers tingled at the memory.

"That's not the same thing as learning how to escape real hunters," Kimba said. "You've done sessions in the predator rooms. It's not the same, is it?"

"No," he admitted. "It's much more dangerous. A wild coyote is a whole different monster from a tame pet canine."

The thought of his beautiful Kimba treed by a coyote with snarling teeth and drooling jaws, even in a controlled situation on the ship, made him dizzy. There had to be other training sessions that would be safer. In his opinion, *all of them* would be safer.

"I'm not sure how useful outdoor training is for you right now," he continued, ready to try a different tack to change her mind. "You don't go outside at all and may never have a mission that involves wild animals. That's not the kind of thing those in the family of the High Command do. The risk is too great. I'm sure there are other lessons that will be more vital and important for your education."

Kimba flared her whiskers at him, but she realized

it was true. After spending a night outside at Turpentine Creek Wildlife Refuge when the rebels transferred her there, she knew she would never volunteer for any missions like that. Outside was terrifying.

"Maybe I've had enough of lions and tigers and ligers and bears and angry beasts for now," she admitted, but she knew in her heart she had missed out on part of her agent training. She'd bring it up again later with her parents.

"You could spend some time learning how the transfer system works," he said, thrilled to the tips of his toes with his brilliant idea.

As the only special agent who had also been a transfer specialist, he was clearly the perfect choice to train Kimba on the basics of the equipment and how it worked. That would ensure the two of them had time together while she was aboard the ship. He held his breath while she considered the idea.

"Yes," she finally said. "I suppose I should know at least a part of how that all works. I've certainly done enough transfers from dangerous situations to appreciate how important it is to the work of an agent. Will you speak to the high commander about it?"

"Absolutely."

"Then that is all for now. I will be back in touch when I know the days of the vacation. Then we can make definite plans for my visit."

"I look forward to it," Thoth said.

He watched Kimba nod and jump down from the counter. She had no idea how much he looked forward to it.

3

PACKING UP

The next day, the giant going-away bags were opened and packing began. Kimba discovered she was more excited for a trip to the ship than she'd expected. At first, she had simply been making the plans she knew Mother expected of her. An agent in her situation should take every opportunity for more training and lessons. But now she realized she really did want to visit the ship and see her cat parents and learn more about the life that a simple mix-up on Earth had taken from her.

Would I have been happier if I had been born on the ship, like I should have been, instead of being adopted by a human family? How different would my life be now?

As she rolled on her back and stretched out lazily on the neatly packed clothes in Mama's suitcase, she knew there were human things she would miss. Nothing on the ship smelled like laundry detergent, fabric softener, and Mama. Kimba rubbed the top of her head back and forth on the clothes to embed that delightful odor into her fur even more.

"Oh, Kimba." Mama sighed as she looked down at her suitcase.

The carefully selected and packed clothes now all had a layer of white cat fur on them. Kimba blinked slowly at her favorite human and rolled to her other side, flailing her legs in the air in the process.

"Are you settling in to join us on the trip, or are you just making a mess?" Mama asked.

Without waiting for an answer, she scooped up the white cat, kissed her on the top of the head, and set her gently on the bed next to the bag. Then she stared at the furry clothes in the suitcase.

"I think the sticky tape roller can take care of that," she said as she started to leave the room.

Then she stopped, looked at Kimba, and went back to close the lid of the bag.

"But let's not have you make it any worse than it is," she said with a chuckle as she headed out of the bedroom to check on Leia's packing progress.

Kimba flicked an ear and stretched out on the bed next to the going-away bag. Then she dug all four sets of claws into the delightful fabric of the suitcase and gave it a few satisfying pulls and rips. She was grateful her own trip to the ship didn't require quite so much planning, but the big bags made excellent scratching posts.

Kimba had figured out that the humans were leaving in the morning. There was an airplane involved, which Daddy and Leia loved but Mama dreaded. Mama always insisted on driving the car anywhere fairly close and for short trips. From the fact that Mama had agreed to get on an airplane and the amount of clothing the family was packing, Kimba was sure they would be gone for several days at least. All the planning and packing and human drama going on had to mean an extended vacation of some sort.

Will they go to the beach again? she wondered. *Is it cold at the beach, or is it always warm there?*

If they went back to Coco Beach, it would be easy to have the same agents watch them and keep tabs on when they headed home.

What were their names? Hurricane. Thunder. Tsumani. And . . .

She couldn't remember the fourth one. That vacation had made her true introduction to ship life possible because no one would miss her at the house for several days—except for Grandma, the petsitter, checking in and making things a bit tricky. What would Mama do for the pets since Grandma was back in Houston and miles and miles away? Who would feed them and put water in the tub?

The Big Black Beast wandered into the bedroom and flopped down on the floor. His ears drooped, and he sighed deeply.

What is more depressing than a sad beast? Kimba

wondered, but she suspected the reason for his sadness.

"Kennel?" Kimba asked.

"Kennel," Max said with another deep sigh. "Soon. I heard them talking about it. I'm getting too old for all that barking and nonsense."

Kimba felt bad for The Big Black Beast, but there wasn't a way to avoid the kennel during a long vacation. The Beast seemed unable to regulate the amount of food he ate at one time—unlike the cats, who could save some food in their bowls for later. And canine creatures don't use litter boxes, so he would have to get outside somehow.

The yard didn't have a fence like the one in Houston, where he'd often stayed outside all day. The Beast tended to run off into the woods around the new house when he got a chance. He'd spent the whole night alone in the forest one time. The kennel was probably the only option for him if the family would be gone for days and days.

"Sorry," she said, not sure what else there was to say.

She was glad the family didn't put the cats in a kennel. It sounded like a smelly, noisy place.

As he had predicted, The Beast was soon loaded into the car and taken to the kennel. Kimba had watched as Mama carefully packed his food, favorite toys, chew bones, and treats. Maybe it wouldn't be that bad for him after all. For some reason Kimba would never understand, he always enjoyed chewing on bones.

The human bags were mostly packed, except for last-minute bathroom things, and Kimba kept both ears perked for as much information as she could gather. She hovered in the corner of the bathroom while Mama and Daddy got ready for bed that night.

"It will be odd to be away for Christmas," Mama said. "But it will be nice to see the family again. It has been too long."

"And there's snow in Michigan," Daddy added. "A white Christmas will be nice."

So, they are going to a place called Michigan . . .

25

and they will be gone for Christmas. Kimba wrapped her tail around her feet as she hunkered down in place. *I wonder what Christmas is like on the ship. Do they celebrate it at all? Do cats exchange gifts?*

Kimba jumped onto the bathroom counter.

"They leave in the morning, if you didn't hear that," she said to the Cat in the Mirror who was most certainly observing. Was it Thoth or some other agent? "Once the coast is clear and I know they are gone, I will make contact."

"Kimba?" Mama called out from the closet, where she was checking for more items to pack. "Are you okay?"

The humans always thought something was wrong when the cats had conversations. Of course, people didn't understand what was being said. Kimba thought that was a good thing.

"She's probably just stressed out about us leaving," Daddy mumbled as he flopped onto the bed. "Hiro is already pouting."

Kimba glanced at her sister, hunkered down on

her pillow on the cedar chest. From the glower on her sister's face, Kimba knew Daddy was right.

She took one last look at the mirror and then hopped down so she could escape the bedroom before Mama shut the door for the night. There was not much worse than being behind a closed door all night long.

Hiro thought suitcases are for pouncing games, not for going away and leaving her alone.

Kimba was sure to mark any suitcase with her fur
so we could be located while we traveled.

VACATION TIME

The next morning, Mama pulled out the special tall cat food bowl that could hold days and days worth of kibble. As the cats ate away at the bottom, more crunchy food would fall into the bowl. A special water contraption that refilled the same way was put on the kitchen floor next to the food bowl.

Kimba and Hiro watched from the counter. It was strange to have food and water on the floor. Normally, The Big Black Beast would gobble it all up immediately. He had zero self-control, so their

29

food was kept up on the counter. But since The Beast was away at a kennel, the cats had full run of the house.

"That should do it until Mindy comes by to check on them," Mama said.

"It's too bad she can't join us," Daddy said as he walked into the kitchen. "It's rough having a job that works twice as hard over the holidays instead of having vacation time."

"I'm just glad she can get away enough to check on things once or twice while we are gone. Finding someone to hire as a petsitter in this small town at such a busy time of year would have been a problem."

"I'll run some water in the tub for Kimba and Hiro," Daddy said. "You know they are not going to drink from that refilling water thingy."

"Depends how thirsty they get, I suppose," Mama said with a glance at the two cats on the counter.

Hiro slow-blinked at Mama, grateful Daddy was putting water in the tub. Drinking from a shared water bowl was disgusting.

The cat sisters watched as their humans fussed around the house for a few more minutes. Then Daddy rolled the big going-away bags from the bedroom and out to the carport.

"Goodbye, babies," Leia said as she staggered out of her bedroom, loaded down with a very full backpack. "I'd give you both twenty hugs and fifty kisses, but then I'd be covered in fur."

Kimba had no interest in hugs or kisses from Leia, though she suspected Miss Fatty Cat had already been smothered in them.

Mama was not so hesitant. Before she tucked into her coat, Mama scooped up Kimba and gave her two kisses on the top of her head.

"You be good, now, and don't get into any trouble. Leave the tree alone. Take lots of naps. We will be home in five days."

While enduring more smothering kisses, Kimba made a mental note: *five days*.

"Goodbye, Hiro," Daddy said as he leaned over and kissed Hiro on the top of the head.

Hiro leaned into the kiss with a head bunt and purred loudly.

Then the humans were bundled up and out the door. Kimba and Hiro watched from the kitchen window as the car pulled down the long gravel driveway and turned off onto the highway.

The house suddenly felt oddly quiet.

"Well, I guess that's it for a few days," Hiro said with a sad sigh. "I'm going to go check on that water in the tub."

As Hiro jumped down, Miss Fatty Cat waddled out of Leia's bedroom and sat down just outside the kitchen.

"Are they gone?" she asked.

"Yes. All gone," Kimba said.

"Okay. Leia is very stressed about this trip. She seems to think I will die while she is gone or something. So many squashy hugs and kisses."

The fat cat could fuss all she wanted, but Kimba knew the truth. Fatty Cat loved every bit of affection she got from her girl.

"I guess I may as well head to the ship," Kimba said as she hopped down from the kitchen counter.

"The ship?" Miss Fatty Cat said. "What are you

going there for?"

"To do some training while the humans are gone and no one will miss me."

"What kind of training could you possibly need? All you will ever do on the ship is look pretty and follow along after your mother. You are the youngest of a long line of cats who run things. You'll never have to do much of anything."

That comment stung. Mother always made it sound like big things would be expected of her, but she also knew that Miss Fatty Cat (aka Agent Onyx) had lived for hundreds of years and knew quite a bit about life on the ship. What if she were right?

"Mother has arranged for some training sessions," Kimba said with a flick of her tail, "and I will take advantage of all of them."

"Suit yourself," Miss Fatty Cat said, "but don't expect you'll ever have much use for it. Maybe some grooming lessons will be helpful to keep that lovely white coat shiny."

Miss Fatty Cat snorted gleefully to herself and then waddled to the basement to take a nap on the game room sofa.

Working her way to the master bathroom mirror, Kimba passed her sister, who was sitting in the tub in the hallway bathroom.

"Is there water?" Kimba asked.

"Yes," Hiro said happily.

"Good. You can have it all to yourself. I'm heading to the ship right now."

"I'll report if there's anything you need to know," Hiro called after her.

Kimba trotted through the bedroom and hopped up on the counter in the bathroom to face the big mirror. Then she straightened up, curled her white tail around her front feet, and stared at her own reflection in the large mirror.

"Greetings," she said. "The humans have gone, and I'm ready to transfer to the ship."

Her reflection shifted and blurred, then the face of her mother appeared. Kimba startled a bit at seeing High Commander Felicity in the mirror. Was there a problem? The white cat gulped and sat up a bit taller.

"Greetings, My Daughter," the high commander

34

said. "It appears you are well and prepared for the transfer."

"Yes, Mother. I am ready."

"Good. Thoth has gone to headquarters to oversee the transfer himself. I'm afraid he is overly concerned every time you use the system. I will patch him in now."

Kimba watched as the high commander tapped on a keyboard. In a moment, Thoth's face appeared in the mirror in a split screen next to Felicity.

"Greetings, Agent Kimba," he said with bright eyes. "Are you ready to come to the ship?"

"Yes, Thoth, I am ready."

"All right then, jump down and sit in the middle of the floor. Give yourself some space from other objects. Do you remember your training?"

"Perfectly. I am calm and focused. When the light flashes, I will start counting."

"Excellent," Thoth said.

He knew she understood what to do, but it seemed professional to ask anyhow. Kimba had made transfers from panicked and dangerous situations. She could certainly follow the rules and transfer safely from the comfort of her Earth home. He watched as she jumped down and settled herself in the middle of the floor. All of the settings on the equipment were ready and waiting for her.

"I'll sign off now," the high commander said. "Thoth will meet you at the transfer platform and escort you to the dining hall for a quick snack. Then you can both meet me in my quarters."

Kimba nodded, and her mother's image faded from the mirror.

"All right, ready?" Thoth asked one last time.

"Ready," Kimba assured him.

She closed her eyes, took a deep breath, and waited. As always, the tingling started in her toes and then spread up along her spine. There was a flash of light, then darkness.

Ten . . . nine . . . eight . . .

5
STRANGE YET FAMILIAR FACE

our . . . three . . . two . . .

Kimba was just beginning to get nervous when she finally felt the cold tile of the transfer platform under her paws.

One.

The trip felt like it had taken longer than usual. Maybe she had counted too fast. It had been a while since she'd made a transfer. She hadn't been on the ship since the rescue mission for Slinky.

When she opened her eyes, she was met with the familiar sight of headquarters and its stark black walls. Looking down from the transfer platform, she spotted the black-and-orange swirled fur of her tortoiseshell friend.

"Greetings," Thoth said, "and welcome back."

"Greetings, and it's nice to be back."

Kimba took a moment to arch her back and stretch out her legs a bit before attempting to walk down the steps. It would have been terribly embarrassing to fall in front of Thoth and all the agents working around them at headquarters.

Once she was down on the main level with Thoth, they turned and headed for the dining hall. Agents peered around their computer monitors or tried to look extra busy as the pair went past. It always took Kimba a while to get used to the ship cats' reactions to her. At home on Earth, she was just a house cat. On the ship, she was royalty. And not just that, she had a unique off-ship life that seemed to fascinate the other agents. Staring was considered rude, but she would often catch their curious gazes before they averted their eyes.

After a quick snack of fresh salmon and some crunchy bits that Thoth called "treats," the pair

38

headed to the high commander's quarters. Walking along past the massive windows that looked out onto space, Kimba was in awe once again. They stopped a couple of times so she could enjoy the view of thousands of stars. Thoth pointed out the small blue ball of Earth in the distance. The idea of actually being in outer space, so far away from home, never ceased to give Kimba a thrill.

As she trotted along next to Thoth through the white hallway, she spotted a familiar cat ahead. They had never officially met, but she remembered him because he'd looked at her differently than any ship cat ever had. Still, she might not have recognized him again if it weren't for his very distinctive markings.

It looked like someone had drawn a line right down the middle of his head—from the nape of his neck, up across the middle of his face, down his nose, and all the way through his chest. On one side of the line, it was pitch black. On the other, it was bright orange. He looked like he had been carefully painted, using edging tape for a perfect line. Kimba had never seen markings like that on any other cat in her whole life.

She had first seen him on her last visit to the ship, when she had done a tour and gone through the nursery and training rooms with Miss Fluffernutter. The tutu-and-tiara-wearing cat had taken Kimba through the kitten rooms and into the instruction rooms, where all the various cats on the ship were learning to do the jobs that their status and family background indicated for the future. Cats from maintenance families were learning how to care for the ship. Cats from transfer backgrounds were learning how to read so they could operate the equipment. Future agents were learning everything they would need to tackle missions on Earth.

That particular orange-and-black cat had been there, working on a computer. No one else in the training room had even glanced up when Kimba peeked in, but he had looked her directly in the eyes. Then he'd *winked* at her. It had been quite startling. Out of respect for the High Command, most cats avoided direct eye contact with her. Not only had this cat made eye contact, but he had winked, like they were friends or something.

All of that flashed through her mind as they passed in the ship hallway. Too late, she realized she was staring at him. The orange-and-black cat looked her directly in the eyes, gave a nod, and winked at her . . . again.

Of all the nerve! She wasn't really sure why it rubbed her fur the wrong way except that it was completely the opposite of the way every other cat on the ship behaved. Maybe he was also part of the High Command and felt like he could be forward and familiar.

As he passed, she noticed his eyes were two different colors as well—one yellow-green and one blue—like hers. Maybe he was her brother. During her visits, she had run into several cats who were related to her, and they were often very calico-looking, like Mother. Or they were black-and-white, like Hiro and Father.

"Who was that?" she asked Thoth. "Is he part of the High Command?"

Thoth looked back over his shoulder and seemed to consider it a moment.

"Oh, that's Janus. He's an agent. I guess he's about twenty. No one from his family is on the High Council or anything like that. Why?"

"He has interesting markings. That line down his face."

She didn't mention the wink. Thoth was very protective of her and might have made a fuss about it. Creating drama when she was on the ship was the last thing on her agenda.

"Yes, it is odd," Thoth agreed. "From what I understand, it's rare. That's where his name comes from. Janus is the name of an old Earth god with two faces. I guess his parents thought it was appropriate."

"Two faces?"

"Yes. I'll show you pictures next time we are on a computer." He stopped in front of the red door that indicated the high commander's quarters. "Here we are."

Thoth pressed the buzzer next to the door, and it quickly swooshed open.

"Greetings!" Commander Griffin called out. "Welcome back, My Daughter!"

He trotted right up to Kimba and rubbed his face along the top of her head. She stood her ground and rubbed back, but his excitement was a bit startling.

Her father was normally more cool and collected.

"Greetings, Agent Thoth," he said when he was done with Kimba. "Good to see you again."

Thoth slow-blinked at the commander. He would never forget the role Commander Griffin had played in allowing him to leave his position as a transfer specialist and become an agent. It was not a popular decision on the ship, but the commander had stood firm. As far as Griffin was concerned, Thoth had saved his daughter's life. Twice. If he wanted to be an agent, by gum, he was going to be an agent.

"Good to see you again, sir," Thoth said.

"Your mother will be here momentarily," Griffin said to Kimba. "She was delayed a bit by some message from another ship."

"I hope it's nothing bad," Kimba said.

"Oh, it's always something," Griffin said, "but it's usually what the humans call a tempest in a teapot. A big fuss over not much of anything. Just some pile of dirty litter they want her to decide on."

Kimba nodded. She often forgot that this ship was not the only cat spaceship in the universe.

High Commander Felicity was in charge of all of them. It was a very impressive and very important job, and Kimba wondered how much of that responsibility would fall on her own white shoulders when she was older and wiser.

"Nothing to worry yourself about," Griffin said as he noticed the concerned look on her face. "Felicity always has it all under her claws."

Kimba sighed and tried to bring her thoughts back to her visit and what she could accomplish while she was there.

"Are there some training sessions planned for me?" she asked.

"Of course," Griffin said. "Thoth, do you have the schedule?"

"I can pull it up on your computer, sir. We arranged some training on the transfer system for this afternoon. It was the easiest to pull together quickly. I can run the training myself, so no one needs to be taken off their jobs. My schedule is flexible." *And mostly revolves around Kimba anyway,* he thought.

"Excellent," Griffin said. "Are you ready to learn a bit about how transfers work, Kimba?"

"Yes, Father."

"I learned all that back in my cadet days," he said, "but I don't remember much about it now. That was over two hundred years ago. Transfers work, and that's all I need to know."

Thoth twisted an ear and shifted his weight a bit. He could never be so calm about what he understood was a dangerous and tricky process. *Maybe it is better not to think about all of that when you are the one being transferred.*

"I am curious about how transfers happen," Kimba said. "I suppose it is good information for every agent. But I am really hoping for some time in the wilderness and combat training rooms. Maybe just with simple creatures that can't kill me. I've faced the outdoors and dangerous beasts. I'd like to be a bit more prepared if that ever happens again."

Thoth felt his hackles rise, and he pursed his whiskers. He thought he'd persuaded her to give up that idea. Commander Griffin narrowed his eyes and flicked an ear.

"Your mother and I don't see any need for you to take part in combat or survival training. As far as we are concerned, you only have a few more years left on Earth. And you live safely there in a warm, cozy house. You should never have to face anything more than that jealous Agent Onyx or that floppy beast. Then you will come back to the ship and take your place here. No combat. No dangerous Earth missions."

Kimba looked back and forth between the two tomcats and realized that neither of them were going to support the idea of her spending one moment in that training room.

"Fine," she said, letting it go for the moment. "Let's start with a lesson on how the transfer process works. Thoth, I believe that is your area of expertise."

"Yes," Thoth agreed warily. Kimba's change of focus had been accomplished much too easily. He was certain they would hear more about the wilderness training room before her visit was complete. "Once we meet with the high commander, we can return to headquarters and begin."

"Perfect!" Griffin said, grateful the subject was changed and back to logical plans. "Thoth can teach you more than any other agent because he has used the transfer system himself. Was quite an expert, from what I've heard. It's good to understand how and why it works so you can avoid accidents or interfering with the system. Let's pull up the rest of your schedule."

As they headed for the computers along a wall of the room, Griffin leaned in closer to Thoth and whispered, "But don't give her *too much* information, if you understand my meaning."

Thoth nodded quickly and glanced at Kimba, who didn't appear to have heard her father's warning. Thoth knew exactly what Commander Griffin was hinting at. If an agent thought too carefully about how many things can go wrong during a transfer, she might never agree to undergo one again. He would avoid the horror stories he had learned in his training. Transfer specialists only experienced the process for themselves once, and that was done in a safe simulation on the ship itself. Transfers away from the ship were only done by agents, and those agents must trust their lives to the system and the technicians who run it.

"I will stick to the important details," Thoth whispered back.

"Good," Griffin said with a flick of his massively fluffy black tail.

Before they made it to the computers, the doors to the room slid open and High Commander Felicity strode in. A pair of impressive Norwegian Forest cat guards remained outside the door, protecting the entrance, and the door slid closed again. Kimba had forgotten that personal guards were one of the new security measures on the ship since the rebels had become more active and had kidnapped her.

"Greetings, My Daughter," Felicity said as she moved forward to touch noses with Kimba.

It was not as physical a greeting as her father had given her, but it was still contact and made Kimba purr quietly. Felicity greeted Thoth with a simple nod.

"Everything taken care of?" Griffin asked.

"Yes, and Atum can handle the rest. Our eldest son is very reliable."

With that settled, she turned to the young cats.

"Now, what do we have planned for our lovely Kimba while she is visiting? Did you already have a snack? Transfers leave one hungry."

"Yes, Mother. Thoth made sure I ate before we came to see you."

"Of course he did."

Thoth loved that the high commander felt she could trust him, especially with Kimba. He slow-blinked at her and then lowered his head in respect.

"We were waiting to see you," Griffin said, "before Kimba headed out for training on the transfer system. Thoth has a whole agenda lined up for her."

"I have sent a message to you that includes the schedule," Thoth added. "It should be waiting for you on your computer."

"Perfect," Felicity said. "I guess it's off with you two, then."

She walked Thoth and Kimba to the door, and once it opened, she spoke to one of the huge guards.

"Francis, please stay with Kimba during her visit on the ship. I'm sure one guard is enough for me over the next few days. Thoth is a good set of eyes, but he will have his own duties during the week. You are assigned to Agent Kimba until she transfers back to Earth."

"Yes, High Commander."

The enormous gray ball of fur and muscles named Francis stood up and nodded at Kimba.

She wanted to say that she didn't need a guard, but if her mother needed one, there didn't seem to be much room for argument. Thoth twitched his whiskers at this addition to their group, but he did not complain either.

"This way back to headquarters," Thoth said and motioned with his head.

Kimba fell into step next to him, and Francis, the gigantic Norwegian Forest cat guard, followed a few steps behind. Mama had often called Kimba a "dainty cat," but she felt like a tiny kitten next to Francis. Her head barely reached his shoulders.

Glancing up at him, she saw that his ears were up and his eyes were alert, even though there was no one but them in the hallway. If she had to have a security guard, he certainly fit the bill.

Felicity and Griffin watched them go and then turned back into the room and shut the door.

"Does that training schedule include time in the wilderness room?" Felicity asked her mate. "I know she has requested that."

"Of course not."

"Good. Let's keep it that way. It can't be long before the rebels discover she's on the ship. That's enough to worry about."

"She's just curious about a part of agent training she did not complete," Griffin said.

"Well, you know what the humans say about curiosity."

"'Curiosity killed the cat,'" Griffin quoted with a twitch of his whiskers.

"Yes. Let's avoid that," Felicity said firmly.

6

TWO-FACED AGENT

Janus checked the hallway to be certain no one had followed him. Then he tapped a code into the control panel next to a small doorway and slipped inside. The room was dark, but his eyes began adjusting immediately.

"Ah, Janus," a cat said. "Greetings and all that. It's good to see you. To what do I owe this visit?"

Janus spotted the outline of the longhaired black cat across the room. She was lying on a large pillow, and her deep-yellow eyes blinked on and off in the darkness.

"Greetings, Commander Horus. I came to inform you that the rumors were correct. Young Agent Kimba is on the ship. I saw her in the hallway with that snotty tortie Thoth."

"Excellent. I'm not sure exactly how her visit can benefit us, but we must find a way."

"Another kidnapping?"

"No." Horus sighed. "That is too risky and would be difficult on the ship. Was she under guard?"

"No. It was just Thoth with her."

"Interesting."

"I've had a thought, Commander Horus."

"I'm all ears," Horus said, twisting her tufted ears back and forth to demonstrate her alertness.

"Young Kimba learned a different set of values growing up on Earth. She has a much more open mind and democratic view of the world. From what I understand, she was pivotal in getting that Thoth into agent training. Based on the rules of our lives and the laws of the High Council, that should have been impossible. There had never been an agent in his family in all of recorded history. Kimba convinced her father, Commander Griffin, and he pushed it through the High Council."

"I agree," Horus said. "That does seem to be how Thoth's promotion came to pass. It is a step in the right direction. A very small step, but exactly what the League For Cat Equality has been hoping for."

"Maybe we can use it to our advantage."

"How so?"

"If I can find a way to impress young Kimba, get on her good side and earn her trust, maybe she can learn to appreciate our goals and plans for cats in the universe and help us. She will have some bit of power as the years go by. High Commander Felicity cannot live forever."

"It certainly feels like she can," Horus said with a swish of her tail. "And her oldest, Commander Atum, is just as set in his ways as she is. Nothing will change when he takes charge."

"But maybe there is hope with the younger generation of the family. The youngest."

"Young Kimba."

"Yes, Commander Horus."

"It's an interesting idea. Do what you can to find out where she will be during her stay, and get her to notice you."

"I've already taken care of the noticing part."

"Ah, good," Horus said. "Then find some way to interact with her. How did that Thoth gain so much trust from the family?"

"Rumor has it he's the one who broke the code and discovered where Senior Transfer Operations Specialist Snowball had hidden Kimba during that kidnapping fiasco. He also transferred down to Earth in the middle of a mission that went wrong and rescued Kimba from an angry beast."

"So, he saved her life."

"Yes, sir."

"Then I suggest you find a way to do that as well."

"Save her life? On the ship?" Janus didn't see how Kimba would end up in a life-threatening situation during the next few days.

"Yes. Create a situation, tactfully and carefully, then save her. And make sure that busybody Thoth is far out of the way so he doesn't do the job for you."

55

Janus sat down and considered the idea. There were not many dangerous places on the ship. Messing with a transfer was too tricky. He didn't know enough about how transfers work to be able to control the situation. They might end up with a dead Kimba. That was not the goal. Too bad Snowball's undercover work had been exposed. He was no use at all in exile down on Earth.

"Do you have any thoughts about how to accomplish this?" Janus asked. "What kind of dangers are there on the ship? *Mild* dangers that I could control and save her from."

"What about the Earth forest training room?"

"The wildlife combat training area?" Janus asked.

"Yes. That sounds perfect. Get her in there with some reasonably dangerous creature and then save her from it."

"How in the world am I going to get young Kimba into the wilderness training room?" Janus said. "I can't imagine her having any interest in that."

7
TRANSFER TECHNOLOGY

Thoth spent several hours walking Kimba through all the steps that went into a successful transfer from the ship to Earth and back again. She had always heard the process took a combination of skill and art to handle the controls and do the complicated math. Now she understood it was true.

"How do you keep from worrying when you press the final button?" she whispered to him when they were between stations. "So many things can go wrong. Thinking about it makes me never want to set foot on that platform again."

"That's why we are doing this training first. You'll have a few days to let the details fade from your mind. Our records of accidents with the transfer system go back millions of years, and the only time something dangerous happens is when the rules are not followed."

"You mean like when an agent is scared and their heart is racing but they transfer anyhow?"

"Yes," Thoth said. "Like that. If your body is doing abnormal things, it throws off the calculations. An agent must be calm. An emergency transfer does happen now and then. Like with you and that angry beast when we were searching for Agent Ebony on Earth. But the specialist at the controls knew you were agitated and made some adjustments."

Thoth thought back to that transfer. It had been a highly dangerous situation. If he had not been down on Earth with her instead of at his transfer post, he would never have allowed anyone else to try it. Transferring a frightened agent was always the worst case a technician could face. He flexed his claws in and out on the black tile floor to shake the memory.

"How often does something bad happen?" Kimba asked. "Do agents ever die in a transfer? They must, now and then. Being an agent is a terribly dangerous job. I don't know why you were so excited to do it."

As he sat down at the next computer station, Thoth pursed his mouth and his whiskers flared. Commander Griffin had been very clear about not scaring his daughter. The conversation was sliding into questions no agent should think about too often.

"It is a dangerous job," he admitted. "Maybe I will regret changing positions on the ship, but I doubt it."

He started typing to bring up her schedule and see what was planned next.

"You didn't answer my question," Kimba said with narrowed eyes.

"What question?"

"About agents dying during a transfer."

"Oh." Thoth shifted his attention from the computer back to her. He would have to give her some answer before they moved on. "I can't tell you that it never happens, but it is very, very rare. Only a few times in recorded history over millions of years. And there were extraordinary things going on. The circumstances were rushed and dangerous. No agent should ever be fearful about making a transfer in a normal situation. What's the number one rule?"

"Never agree to the transfer if you are not ready."

"Correct. A normal transfer is not dangerous."

"Then why do you always insist on being involved in my transfers?"

Thoth looked back at the computer screen to avoid eye contact.

"What do you mean?" Thoth said.

"You always want to know when I'm coming and going, and you are always there when I arrive. It's like you don't trust the other technicians to do it right. Or don't you trust me?"

"Of course I do but—"

Francis the guard moved in their direction, saving Thoth from having to explain the real reason he was so protective of her.

"Agent Kimba," Francis said, "are you ready to move to your next scheduled training, or would you prefer a brief break? Your regular visitor quarters have been prepared. The high commander is concerned that you not overdo it today. When was your last rest time?"

Kimba saw Thoth's pupils widen, and she was startled by the guard's question as well. Her tail twitched. *Does he think I can't handle my own nap schedule?*

"It has been a few hours," she said, trying to be polite, "but I am fine for now. What's next on the agenda?"

"You are set to visit the grooming center," Thoth said. "Just as an observer, of course. But I can schedule a grooming session for you while you are here if you would like."

"There's a grooming center?" *I thought Miss Fatty Cat was joking about that.*

An image raced through her mind of The Big Black Beast coming home from the groomer in the summer with all of his fur shaved off to practically nothing. Being shaved always made him extra wiggly and excited, but it sounded like a nightmare to Kimba. She certainly hoped they didn't shave cats on the ship.

"Some cats need help with keeping their hygiene up to standards," Thoth explained. "Especially older cats or those who are sick. And cats with thick or long hair."

Kimba and Thoth both looked over at Francis. He cocked his head and then understood their un-asked question.

"My fur is both extremely long and extremely thick," he said, "but I rarely need assistance. And I have a mate who is diligent in both of our groom-ing. We do visit the center, however, a few times a year. It can be very relaxing. Rather like what humans call a spa."

Kimba wasn't sure what a spa was. Did her humans have one? They accomplished all of their grooming in the bathroom. It involved lots of soap and water. Would the ship's grooming center want to give her a bath in water? With soapy suds? She shivered at the thought of it and felt her hackles rise.

"I think I'll just observe during this visit," she said. "I don't need help with my grooming, and I've never had another cat do it for me."

"Not even your mother?" Thoth asked.

Then he clamped his mouth shut. He laid back his ears and thrashed his tail, not sure how to correct that thoughtless comment. He wanted to dig a hole in the black tile floor and hide himself for a week. Of course Kimba's mother couldn't have groomed her. They had been separated as soon as Kimba and her sister were born.

"Well, no," Kimba said, not as upset as Thoth expected her to be. "At least not that I remember. I guess the human female, Mama, helped Hiro and me some in those first few days before our eyes were open. And sometimes when we were kittens and got messy learning to eat. Hiro has groomed me a bit, but that was mostly just to be social. A few licks to my head. Otherwise, I take care of myself."

Then she suddenly remembered the day when she was only a year old. She had just learned about the Cats in the Mirror and accomplished her second mission from Special Agent Regalus—to escape outside. Mama had helped clean her up after that horrible day. So much grass and dirt. That had been one of the most embarrassing experiences of her life. She didn't want to mention it. Not even to Thoth.

Thinking of Mama made her wonder if the family was having a safe airplane flight and a good Christmas wherever they were. It was so strange to be apart from them at the biggest holiday time of the year.

Thoth suspected that Kimba was thinking about having missed out on time with her birth mother, and he shifted in agitation at having needlessly upset her.

"So we're going to the grooming salon?" Francis asked, either ignoring the tense situation or not noticing it in the first place.

"Yes," Thoth said. "Lead the way, please."

Francis headed out across the open section of headquarters, and Kimba followed him. Thoth trailed behind. He hoped the feeling would pass, but he found it uncomfortable to walk next to his

Kimba at that moment in time.

Agents along the way pretended not to stare and averted their eyes, as usual, while the three cats trotted from the dark room and into the bright-white hallways of the ship.

8

BUBBLES AND PAINTED NAILS

Kimba rolled over on a pillow in her guest quarters and wondered how long she'd been asleep. Without a window and the light of the sun, it was impossible to tell if it was night or day. She stretched out all four legs, flexed her claws, and yawned, her pink tongue curling at the end.

She was supposed to press the red button next to the computer to let Thoth know when she was awake. But what if he was still resting? She decided to wait a bit longer and enjoy the quiet. It was nice to be alone for a bit with no one guarding her or pretending not to gawk at her.

The visit to the grooming salon had been interesting. Sadly, she had seen one cat being shaved. He was a flat-faced Persian, and it took every ounce of Kimba's self-control not to laugh at him.

All the long white fur on his body had been shaved down to nothing more than peach fuzz, except for his head and tail. Those two bits were still fluffy and enormous compared to his body. It looked like he would fall face-first from the weight of his head if he tried to stand up. He reminded her of a weird-looking lion wannabe with a puffy mane. Or a fancy poodle beast. Or one of the Funko Pop toys that Daddy collected with heads four times the size of their bodies. She'd clenched her jaw to keep the laughter inside, but her ears and nose flushed almost red with the effort.

Thoth had noticed her blushing and hoped she could contain herself. Some ridicule might encourage the tomcat to care for himself better in the future, but being laughed at by a member of the High Command family would have been the worst kind of embarrassment. No ship cat deserved that. So Thoth quickly explained that shaving the Persian was the easiest solution to badly matted fur. Brushing out all of those knots would have been painful.

"Of course, a respectable cat should never let his fur get that matted in the first place," he'd whispered through pursed whiskers before hurrying her along to the next station.

There were tubs for human-style baths with soap and water, but Thoth assured her those were only used for very old or sick cats. Kimba was glad no one was getting a bath because a miserable, soaking-wet cat would have been too hilarious to keep to herself.

Most of the stations involved brushing or toenail clipping. One extremely fluffy gray cat was having the tufts of fur between her toes trimmed. Kimba imagined having that much fur between your toes would be annoying, and maybe even downright dangerously slippery on the tile floors of the ship.

In another section of the salon, two tawny Siamese cats were having their claws painted orange. Kimba had seen the girls do that to their fingernails at home on Earth, but the salon cat had to use her teeth to hold the brush. Kimba thought it looked like a tricky business, but the technician never got one drop of polish on their fur. It reminded Kimba of Miss Fluffernutter and her pink-painted claws. Seeing Siamese cats also made her wonder about Agent Artemis, her second Cat in the Mirror contact.

Is he on the ship or off on some mission? She'd have to ask about him later.

After the grooming salon visit, Francis had insisted that Kimba take a rest. She had not argued, though Thoth had looked a bit unhappy about it. She imagined he probably had more planned on her schedule.

On the way to her guest quarters, the three of them had walked past some very large green double doors. Kimba had never seen anything like that on the ship before. There was a giant window looking into the room, so she trotted up to it and put her front paws on the ledge so she could see inside. What lay beyond the extra-thick layer of glass took her breath away.

Below her was a forest, just like outside the windows at home. There were tall trees of all shapes and varieties, and there was grass on the ground and even a winding river running through it all. Large boulders were scattered around the huge space, and artificial sunlight poured down over all of it. From the window, Kimba looked down on the treetops, like the room itself was actually two or three levels below her. It was so vast, she couldn't see the walls on the other three sides. Only forest.

That room must be five times the size of head-quarters, she thought. It was hard to wrap her head around how huge the whole ship must be with a million cats on board and enormous rooms like that all over the place. *But why is there a forest on the ship?*

Francis glanced through the window briefly, then he continued on.

"It doesn't look like there are any training exercises going on during this shift," he said. "Maybe we can schedule to watch one later."

Thoth cleared his throat loudly, and Kimba wondered if he had the start of a nasty fur ball.

"What happens in there?" she asked.

"That's the wilderness and predator combat training room," Francis said without turning around.

Kimba had felt the fur along her spine prickle.

Now, in the comfort of the guest quarters, she wondered why that wilderness room was so fascinating to her. She had hated being outside, even in the city with nothing but some birds and hot weather to worry about. Her home in Arkansas was in the middle of the woods. She'd heard Mama talk about coyotes and bobcats and bears and snakes. Kimba remembered the bear she'd met at Turpentine Creek Wildlife Refuge. He seemed nice enough, but he was behind bars.

What was his name? Oh yes, Bam Bam.

It had been terrifying to be outside in that forested big cat refuge all night long. She had hidden in the hole of a concrete block and listened to the lions chat from their enclosures.

"Hooorrr, hooorrr, hooorrr," they had caroled long into the night.

The sounds of the lions, tigers, and even a coyote and a monkey had been unnerving.

Why am I so fascinated with facing the outside again? She had no logical answer.

Out of the corner of her eye, she noticed the red button on her computer was flashing on and off. Deciding it must be a signal for something, she slunk from her comfy pillow and pressed the button. The computer screen flickered, and then High Commander Felicity's image appeared.

"Greetings, My Daughter. I hope you had a nice rest."

"Yes, thank you."

"Your father and I will be meeting shortly in the dining hall for a light meal before we start our shift. Why don't you join us before your next training session?"

"That sounds good," Kimba said, realizing she was definitely hungry.

"Excellent. I'll alert Francis to escort you."

She was about to object that Francis wasn't necessary, but her mother's image faded before she could respond. Kimba had no idea how to get to the dining hall, so maybe it was just as well that Francis could show her the way.

She did a quick groom of her fur and visited the odd bathroom situation, more like a human toilet than an Earth litter box. As she considered what else to do before heading to dinner, there was a scratch at the door.

"Come in," she called out.

The door slid open, but the entrance was blocked by the massive gray furry body of Francis. Kimba tipped her head to look up at him, and he twisted one ear to the side—listening to some noise down the hallway.

"This door should be locked. And you should never blindly open the door when someone scratches," he said firmly. "It could be anyone. Even a rebel."

Kimba's tail lashed. He was right, of course, but she didn't like to be reminded of it.

"Remember, use this to check," Francis said, touching a screen next to the door. "It will show you who is in the hallway. And keep your door locked when you are in your room."

"Yes. I understand. Sorry," she mumbled.

"Are you ready to go, Agent Kimba?"

She nodded, and Francis moved aside to allow her to pass. When the door closed behind her, he used a claw to type a code of six numbers into a keypad next to the door.

"So no one can get in and be waiting for you when you return," he said.

Kimba swallowed a lump in her throat. Had things gotten more dangerous with the rebels since she had been on the ship before? There seemed to be so many security worries now. She would ask Mother about it at dinner.

With Francis one step ahead, the two of them headed for the dining hall.

Down the hallway behind them, a door slid open. Janus peeked out and watched them walk away.

9

REQUEST DENIED

The dining hall was a mass of colorful fur and swishing tails. Kimba and Francis stopped at the entrance for a moment. She tried not to stare, but she had never seen the room so full of activity. Then the sea of cats seemed to magically part and High Commander Felicity sauntered toward them. Her guard cat stood at attention behind her.

"It's always busier at shift change while the crew grab a meal before their rest period," Felicity said.

She led Kimba to the area of cushions and low

tables reserved for her family and the High Council at the far end of the room. It was up on a little riser, so they had a view of the whole dining hall. Of course, no one looked their way.

Felicity's guard sat down at one end of the space and Francis took up a position at the other end while they waited for their food to arrive. Kimba watched as Francis's whiskers twitched and his ears swiveled back and forth. Who would dare approach with them on duty?

Carts covered in plates of food arrived quickly, and several gray tabby cats set to work placing servings in front of Kimba, the high commander, Commander Griffin, and the rest of the cats seated there. There were six other cats in the area, all with long tawny and dark-brown fur—like her mentor, Special Agent Medusa Gloriosa. But the blue-ribbon-winning show cat wasn't one of them. Medusa was still enjoying her red-velvet-cushioned retirement on Earth.

The Himalayan cats had nodded politely when Kimba and her parents sat down, but they seemed to be having some sort of private meeting. Mother didn't introduce them. Kimba realized she had probably met them before when she reported to the High Council.

A plate covered in brown bite-sized bits of something she didn't recognize was placed in front of her. Meals on the ship were usually fish. She gave it a quick sniff, but she still couldn't place it. She didn't want to be rude, so she speared a piece with her claw and popped it into her mouth. It was quite delicious, but she'd never tasted anything like it.

"Mouse," Griffin said.

"What?"

"It's mouse. We have a whole breeding facility here on the ship."

Kimba swallowed with some difficulty. She'd never eaten a mouse before. She'd never even seen one, though she sometimes heard them scrabbling around in the walls of their house in the country.

"Would you like to visit the mouse farm while you're here?" Griffin asked between bites.

A whole giant room full of mice? Kimba couldn't decide if that was interesting or horrifying.

"I think my schedule is already pretty full," she said.

Griffin shrugged and popped another mousy bite into his mouth.

Then an idea crossed her mind. Mama always told the girls to wait until Daddy had supper before asking him for anything or trying to share news with him. Now here was her own father with a belly full of mouse. Maybe it was a good time to bring up the forested training room again. Once she'd seen how amazing it was, her desire to get into the room had quadrupled.

"Father," she said, spearing another brown bit of food, "what I still really want to do is visit that wilderness training room. I got a peek at it when we passed by earlier, and it looks fascinating."

"Um . . . ," Griffin said.

"Do you think you could add it to my training?"

Griffin sighed. "We've already talked about this, Kimba. There's really no need for that."

Kimba knew she was going to have to skitter around his worries, like she had seen Mindy and

Leia do with Daddy when they really wanted something but he had already said no.

Act sad, she thought. *Heartbroken.* The girls tended to get teary, but that wouldn't work in the cat world. Instead, she let her whiskers droop and sighed sadly.

"I know," she said quietly. "But all those trees were so tall and beautiful. I've never been able to climb a tree before."

Griffin glanced at her and shifted his whiskers.

Does that mean he's thinking about it? Then she had the spark of an idea for another way to convince him.

"Some of those trees look just like the Christmas tree at home," she said. "It made me quite homesick to see them down in that big room with no decorations or anything. So lonely."

She dropped her head and sighed again.

Griffin cleared his throat and was about to answer when the high commander stood up and both guards leaped to attention. The other cats at the table turned to stare at Felicity as well.

"The High Council meets in ten minutes," she said, turning to Kimba. "They are expecting a standard report from you."

Kimba forgot all about the forest room and felt the hackles rise all along her back and up her neck. Her tail puffed, and her ears flushed bright pink.

"I'm giving a report to the high council?"

"Of course," her mother said. "Just like every visit."

With that, Felicity stalked out of the dining hall. Griffin popped his last few bites of mouse into his mouth and trotted after her, still chewing. Kimba knew she was supposed to follow as well. She glanced at Francis, and he looked at her expectantly. She sighed and padded her way down from the seating area.

As the mass of cats in the aisle parted for them and pretended not to notice them at the same time, Kimba thought she saw the two-toned face of Janus. The ranks of many-colored cats closed up behind her before she could be sure.

10

KITTENS IN TRAINING

After Kimba's report to the High Council, Thoth joined her for a trip to the nursery. That was one part of the visit Kimba had been looking forward to. Francis was allowed a break during this shift because there couldn't possibly be dangerous rebels hiding in the nursery rooms.

Miss Fluffernutter met them at the bright-pink door and proudly ushered them inside her domain.

"We are so honored to have you back in the nursery, Kimba," Miss Fluffernutter gushed.

She led Thoth and Kimba through the grand entrance, where the ceiling was covered with sparkling stars. Then she paused and spun around dramatically, her pink tutu moving in harmony with her fluffy fur.

"I'm so sorry! *Agent* Kimba."

Fluffernutter gave a little bow, and her tiara tipped precariously toward her nose. Kimba stifled a laugh. She dipped her head slightly at the nursery matron, as she had seen High Commander Felicity do in situations like that. Fluffernutter looked relieved to be forgiven and turned back to her tour-guide duties.

They peeked into the newborn nest, but all the tiniest kittens were sleeping peacefully. Moving to the next room, Kimba was met with a horde of tumbling, frolicking puffs of fur.

"Kittens, rally on the line!" Miss Fluffernutter commanded.

The little ones did their best, but there was quite a bit of stumbling and knocking into each other and falling down. Kimba suspected some of that bumbling was on purpose and had more to do with being silly kittens than it had to do with being young and awkward. As with her first visit to that section of the ship, Kimba was charmed by the tiny balls of fluff and their efforts to be formal and proper.

How would my life be different if I had been born on the ship? she wondered. *Would Hiro and I have grown up in this nursery room?*

When all of the kittens were mostly organized on the pink line at the front of the room, Fluffernutter addressed them formally.

"Kittens, please welcome Agent Kimba."

"Greetings, Agent Kimba," the kittens all chanted in unison.

"Agent Kimba is the youngest daughter of High Commander Felicity," Miss Fluffernutter said with a toss of her tiara-laden head.

"Ooooo," the kittens all mewed, quite impressed.

Then they all stared expectantly at the tortoise-shell cat standing next to Kimba.

"Um, yes. And this is Thoth," Fluffernutter mumbled.

"*Agent* Thoth," Kimba corrected, feeling her tail puff.

"Yes, yes. Agent Thoth," the nursery matron said.

"Greetings, Agent Thoth," the kittens chorused.

Trying to ignore Fluffernutter's downright rude introduction of Thoth, Kimba thought back on what Mother had said to the impressionable kittens on her last visit.

"It is an honor to meet all of you," Kimba said. "I'm sure you are studying diligently and will make all of your families proud for generations to come."

From the proud twinkle in Fluffernutter's eyes, that had been the right thing to say. She nodded approvingly and dismissed the kittens, who immediately rushed off in a tussle of fur and claws.

As the trio moved through the training rooms, Kimba remembered that this was where she had begun to fully understand how life on the ship worked. Cats were trained in the same jobs as their parents and their grandparents before them. No one tried to stray or challenge the system without being called a rebel and a danger to other cats.

Except her.

She had convinced her parents to let Thoth change careers. Did that make her a bit of a rebel as well? She wasn't sure how she felt about that.

Miss Fluffernutter clearly isn't thrilled about it.

The guardian of the nursery might not have meant to drop the "agent" from Thoth's name, but she had added it back with a definitely sour attitude. Maybe she didn't like the altering of the destiny of a kitten she had raised and trained. Kimba and Thoth had messed up the organized system.

Instead of going through the kitchen training area, Miss Fluffernutter headed down a hallway Kimba had not seen before. She stopped in front of a large window, and Kimba peered into a room where kittens were learning how to use a litter box.

"This area is only for future agents, of course," Miss Fluffernutter said. "Ship cats don't have to fuss with litter, but life in most Earth homes requires its efficient use."

Kimba watched as one very industrious kitten attempted to cover a pretend "mess"—using every

85

inch of the litter in her assigned box. With her eyes tightly closed, the kitten kicked at the litter, one back paw at a time, spraying it everywhere around her in great waves.

Whoosh, the litter flew to the right.

Whoosh, the litter flew to the left.

Whoosh, a big glob of it headed toward where Kimba stood at the window.

"No, no, no!" The gray shorthaired cat in charge scolded her. "That's too much! Just use your front paws to gently scoop and bury."

The kitten hesitated and opened her eyes. She looked at the mess around her box and then up at the teacher.

"Sorry," she mewed.

But Kimba noticed, when the teacher looked away, there was a gleeful sparkle in that kitten's eyes that could only be pride in the disaster area of litter she had created.

Kimba sighed. Maybe if she had been trained in how to use a litter box properly she wouldn't avoid it and use the bathroom sink instead. Hiro hated

litter even more. She fussed that it got stuck between her toes. She preferred to use the bathroom
sink too. They both used the box sometimes, but it
wasn't their first choice.

Poor Mama, Kimba thought. Mama hated it when
they went potty in the sink, but at least they didn't
make a littery mess like the kittens in that training
room.

Kimba watched as another kitten obediently
attempted to bury an item by gently moving the
litter around with her front paw, like the teacher
had said. But she never quite got the pile of litter
over the object she was supposed to cover, even
though it seemed like she had shifted every grain in
her efforts to be tidy.

"Break time," the teacher called out.

Dozens of kittens all leaped from their litter
boxes, spraying piles of sandy mess every which
direction, and rushed for a table of snacks at the
back of the room.

Thoth chuckled. Kimba wondered if he had
gone through some litter training when he became
an agent. Since a transfer technician was never

supposed to leave the ship, that wouldn't have been part of his normal kitten education.

Miss Fluffernutter sighed, probably grateful she wasn't responsible for cleaning up the mess the kittens had made. Then she headed down the hallway and around a bend into an area Kimba recognized.

As they walked past the diplomat training room, Kimba recalled seeing Janus in there so many months ago. He'd been working on a computer. And he'd winked at her. She felt her fur rankle at the thought of it.

Maybe some agents are more self-assured than others.

"Would you like to complete some lessons while you are here, Agent Kimba?" Miss Fluffernutter asked, stopping at that doorway. "I'm sure Thoth did a lovely job of your tutoring—as much as could be expected from someone who is not trained to be a teacher. You passed your exams with honors. But there is always more to learn."

Kimba looked at Thoth, worried he would be offended again, but he just slow-blinked a *whatever* in return.

"We will see what fits into her schedule," Thoth said. "It is unclear when she will have to return to Earth."

"Of course," Miss Fluffernutter said. "Of course."

"Do you have any information about the Christmas holidays on Earth?" Kimba asked.

Thoth looked surprised, but Miss Fluffernutter appeared to ponder this.

"I would imagine so," she finally said. "It wouldn't be in the required round of lessons, but I'm sure research has been gathered over the years. I will have one of our teachers put together some files for you, in case you have time to study during your visit."

"Thank you," Kimba said with a nod, positive Fluffernutter would consider studying to be the most important thing an agent could do.

Before they could discuss it further, a shorthaired black cat trotted up.

"Greetings," he said with a nod at all of them. Then he turned to Kimba. "Agent Kimba, we need you to sign in to the nearest computer immediately. Your sister is at her mirror with an urgent report."

"Hiro?" Kimba gasped. "Is she okay?"

**Hiro, on the wood stove
with everyone's Christmas stockings.**

11
UNEXPECTED VISITORS

Hiro heard the thunk of the deadbolt on the back door. She lifted her head and froze. Then she heard the door creak open and the odd noise of canine toenails scrabbling on the mudroom floor.

Are they back already? Hiro wondered. It had only been two days.

"Kimba? Hiro? Miss Fatty Cat?" a voice called out. It sounded like Mama, but not quite right at the same time.

Then there was a whimpering and the bark of a beast. Definitely not The Big Black Beast. An unknown creature was in the house. The hackles rose along Hiro's back, and her black tail puffed. The tuxedo cat lowered herself flat out on her pillow on the cedar chest and folded her ears down against her head. Was it better to run and hide or stay put and hope not to be noticed?

She heard the familiar plunk of a stack of mail being dropped on the kitchen counter. Then, in a bluster of winter coat and wiggling beast body, Mindy and a strange animal burst into Mama and Daddy's room. They stopped near the door when they saw Hiro.

"Hey, Hiro. There *you* are, at least," Mindy said. "Where are the others?"

Mindy hadn't lived in the house since she had become a grown-up human and moved out, but Mama had mentioned that Mindy would stop by to check on them. However, bringing an invading creature with her was unacceptable. Hiro let her feelings be known with a low, menacing growl.

"Oh, Hiro, you're so silly."

Instead of leaving, Mindy came around the bed toward Hiro on her pillow, and the wiggling ball of fur followed behind her. Hiro tried to flatten out more, but it didn't help. Mindy patted her right on the head. But that wasn't the worst of it. The strange beast—that brown-and-black blur of fur—came up and touched noses with her.

Hiro sneezed, shook her head, and scooted back on the pillow as far as she could. The Big Black Beast knew better than to make physical contact with her. Why didn't this new waggly monster understand the rules?

"Hiro, this is Dottie. She lives with Slinky and me now. Can you say hello?"

Hiro had no intention of saying hello.

"Hello, kitty cat!" Dottie yipped with great glee. "It's very nice to meet you."

Hiro's response was a long, slow hiss. "Hhhhkkk."

"Oh, Hiro. You're such a poop," Mindy said.

Dottie tipped her head, confused. She'd never been hissed at before. Not sure how to react or what it meant, she decided the wisest course of action was to plow ahead and ignore it.

"Where is the Miss Fatty Cat one?" Dottie asked. "I'm supposed to tell her that her sister says hello and that everything is fine. Well, except for the fact that I moved into the house. Hah!"

Dottie held her mouth open in a canine laugh, but Hiro was unimpressed.

"Slinky's sister is probably in the other room," Hiro said sharply. "In Leia's bedroom."

"Come on, Dottie," Mindy said, not understanding the conversation. "Let's go check on the others and get their food and water refilled."

Dottie spun in a circle. Her fluffy tail slashed wildly and whapped Hiro in the face. Then the creature followed at Mindy's heel out of the room.

"I suppose we should clean out the litter boxes too," Mindy said as she left.

Dottie hopped around three times, like that was the most amazing thing any human had ever said in the history of the world.

Hiro glared after them and watched out the door as the pair entered Leia's bedroom.

"Hello, Miss Fatty Cat," Mindy said.

"Oh, Miss Fatty Cat!" Dottie barked excitedly. "Your sister says hello and that life is wonderful and that you should put together a chat with your parents for Christmas. Doesn't that sound like fun?"

Dottie's message was met with a hiss and a low rumble. The fat cat was quite expert at angry yowls and grumbling noises. Hiro wondered if she had even listened to the message or just reacted to the stranger in her bedroom territory.

"Man." Mindy laughed. "Y'all are grumpy today."

Hiro could hear the girl refilling food bowls and cleaning litter boxes. Mindy also ran some fresh water in the bathtub, which made the tuxedo cat happy. Then the girl and the beast clumped downstairs to take care of things on that level of the house.

"Kimba?" Mindy called out. "Kimba?!"

Hiro felt a nervous flutter. There was no way to get her sister back so Mindy could see her. *How can I even communicate what is going on?* She could just run over and report in the mirror. But how would they get Kimba to the control room and transferred that quickly? She could be anywhere in the ship, even asleep or in training.

Mindy came back in the master bedroom and stooped down to look under the bed. Then she looked up over the top of the mattress at Hiro.

"Where's your silly sister?"

Hiro just stared at the girl.

"Well," Mindy said, standing up again, "I guess she's around here somewhere. It's not like she could have gotten outside or anything. Grandma used to complain about how she could never find you guys when she did the petsitting. Hmmm."

As Mindy considered where Kimba could be, Dottie waggled her way back into the room. Her fluffy tail thrashed and swirled, and it made Mindy smile. She grabbed the creature with a hand on each side of her furry face and gave her a kiss on the forehead. That made Dottie so happy, she just collapsed on the floor, belly up, and wiggled on her back. Watching Dottie made Hiro want to take a nap. *Exhausting.*

"That's it, then," Mindy said, rubbing Dottie's belly

and then standing up and looking at Hiro. "Mail is picked up. Food and litter boxes taken care of. I even put some fresh water in the tub for you and Kimba, you spoiled cats, you."

Hiro was grateful for the water refill, though she didn't appreciate being called spoiled.

"I'll be back in a day or so to check on you again. Probably on Christmas Day, since I at least get that day off from work."

Mindy considered going back over to give Hiro a pet or a hug, but then she thought better of it. Hiro didn't much appreciate that kind of thing, unless it was from Daddy.

"Bye, then," she said instead and headed for the back door. "And Merry Christmas!"

"Yeah, Merry Christmas!" Dottie barked, even though she had no idea what that meant. She hadn't been alive long enough to celebrate Christmas before.

The door opened and clunked shut again, and the dead bolt clicked into place. Listening carefully, Hiro could hear a car door opening and shutting as

Dottie and Mindy got in. Then there was the crunching of tires on the gravel driveway as they drove off.

After a minute to be sure they were really off the property, Hiro relaxed and sighed.

"Are they gone?" Miss Fatty Cat called out.

"Yes, I think so."

"Mindy has a lot of nerve, bringing that beast into our house."

"Did you hear the message from Slinky about talking to your parents?"

Miss Fatty Cat was silent for a moment. Then she said, "Yes, I heard it. I suppose it's the right thing to do."

A holiday conversation with her hyper, over-protective mother was not top on Miss Fatty Cat's agenda, but if Slinky was up for it, she would join in and help guide the conversation away from when they would both return to the ship. If mother saw they were safe and happy, maybe she could relax for a bit. Maybe.

"I'm going to report about this visit to Kimba,"

Hiro said. "Do you want to talk with the Cat in the Mirror to set up the call with your parents?"

There was no immediate answer, but then Hiro heard the clump of the fat black cat jumping down from the bed. Assuming she was headed to the mirror, Hiro jumped down daintily and trotted into the bathroom. She hopped up on the counter and heard the click-click-click of Miss Fatty Cat's claws on the wood floor behind her. Her tail twitched in annoyance.

Why can't that cat care for her claws like she should? It sounds like a beast clicking along.

"Greetings," Hiro said to the mirror, trying to ignore Miss Fatty Cat's lazy grooming habits. She needed to focus on all the proper manners expected during mirror communications. This was usually Kimba's job.

In a moment, her reflection in the mirror became wavy and then vanished as the image of Special Agent Artemis appeared.

"Greetings, Hiro." The Siamese cat nodded his head quickly to acknowledge Hiro and then tapped away at a few keys. "One moment, please. Let me find

Thoth and Kimba and patch you through to them as well."

"Thank you. Something just happened that I need to tell them about. Mindy and some strange beast stopped by, and Mindy was a bit upset she couldn't find Kimba."

As Artemis appeared to be waiting to hear from Thoth and Kimba, Miss Fatty Cat cleared her throat. The tawny cat peered over Hiro's shoulder and spotted the black cat sitting there.

"Ah, Agent Onyx. Greetings."

"Greetings, Special Agent Artemis. I also have a communication for you."

"Yes?"

"My sister, Agent Ebony, would like to coordinate a conversation with our parents during the human Christmas holiday. The Wiggly Black Beast that lives with her delivered the message to me today when Mindy came to visit."

"You want to speak with your mother?" Artemis asked. He was careful not to add, *Really?* His hackles rose a bit at the thought of Demeter in the control room.

"Yes. I think it would be best. My side of things will be quite clear with the humans out of town, but can you please check with Ebony and see when her apartment is free?"

"Of course," Artemis said. "I'll will pass the message on to the agent monitoring her mirror and speak with your parents about it."

That was a conversation he didn't look forward to at all.

"Thank you." She flicked an ear, then realized she had nothing else to say. "I'll leave you to it, Hiro."

She waddled and click-clacked out of the room to munch on some of the fresh food Mindy had left.

Hiro's attention was drawn back to the mirror again as the faces of Thoth and Kimba appeared in a split screen next to Artemis.

"Greetings, Hiro!" Kimba said. "It's always so funny to be on this side of the mirror and see our house like the agents see it all the time. Is everything okay? They said it was urgent."

"No, no," Hiro said. "Nothing urgent. Everything's fine. I just wanted to let you know that Mindy stopped by today to check on us, like Mama said she would. She brought a strange beast with her. That was not pleasant at all. I'm pretty sure Mama didn't know that would happen. The creature touched noses with me. It was disgusting. Anyhow, Mindy seemed a bit upset that she couldn't find you, but she said she would look again when she comes back in a couple of days, on Christmas Day."

"Is Christmas in a day or two?" Kimba asked, surprised.

Artemis looked at his computer monitor and tapped a couple of keys.

"The humans will celebrate Christmas Eve to-morrow night. Then Christmas is the next day," he announced.

"It will be strange not to have any Christmas music or special food or gifts or anything," Hiro said. "Are you having a party on the ship?"

"I don't know," Kimba admitted. "I didn't realize it was happening so soon."

"I'm sure arrangements can be made," Thoth said, thinking quickly. "We can certainly pull something together. It can be a lesson on Earth celebrations and customs for the agents who have never enjoyed Christmas on the planet."

If his Kimba wanted Christmas, he would find a way to give her Christmas.

"Interesting," Artemis said. "I'll make a note for the high commander. Maybe different agents who have served around the world can share their experiences."

"That sounds fascinating," Kimba said. "Is Christmas different, depending on where you live on Earth?"

"Oh yes," Artemis said, "from what I have witnessed through the mirrors over the years. While some traditions are similar, others are quite different. And the way the holiday has been celebrated over the decades and centuries of human existence has changed as well. Most recently, I've noticed that the special music and decorations begin earlier and earlier in the calendar year each season."

"I've heard Mama talk about that," Kimba said. "She is very insistent there are no decorations in the house until after the turkey day. Daddy usually puts the tree up that night when the dishes are done."

Hiro's tail swished at the thought of Daddy. Was he safe? Her back started to jump and twitch, so she took a deep breath and tried to settle down. Having a fight with her tail in front of Special Agent Artemis and Agent Thoth would be embarrassing.

"Getting back to the subject of your report," Artemis said to Hiro, "do you feel Kimba will need to return for that next visit from Mindy?"

Kimba's eyes narrowed. She had quite a bit more planned for this visit to the ship, including getting into that wilderness training room. Ending it early would be quite annoying.

"No," Hiro said. "I think it will be fine. Just make sure you monitor the mirror. Then you should hear if there is a problem, or I can alert you. We've snuck back into the house before when the grandmother was trying to find us. I suppose Kimba can do it again if necessary."

Good, Kimba thought. *I'm not nearly ready to head back to Earth.*

**The Wiggly Black Beast (Dottie)
in her holiday bandanna.**

12

OPPORTUNITY KNOCKS

Kimba had napped and felt much better. For a house cat who normally spent huge chunks of the day sleeping, Kimba was feeling a bit overwhelmed by the demands of the schedule on the ship. Maybe Francis had been right to be worried about her getting enough rest. She stretched her legs and arched her back as high as it would go.

Kimba had requested a brief nap after answering questions in front of the high council for what seemed like forever and being formal and proper in the nursery rooms. All those serious cat faces staring at her—it was unnerving. And all the effort to be polite and dignified and careful about answering in just the right way was exhausting.

It had been nice to talk to Hiro, though she was glad she didn't have to return home quite yet. It was strange to think, in a few years that might be the only way she ever saw her sister—through the mirror in the human house. Hiro would choose to go back with Daddy and live undercover on Earth, no question about it. Kimba was pretty sure High Commander Felicity wouldn't offer her that option.

Kimba was just finishing a quick grooming session before calling Thoth when she heard a scratch at the door. Maybe he was checking on her. Or maybe someone had come to wake her up and get her moving. She remembered what Francis had said about checking the hallway through the monitor, so she pressed the button.

Then she gasped. It was definitely not Thoth or her parents or Francis.

She could see a two-tone-faced cat sitting patiently outside her door. It could only be Janus. She hesitated. *What in the world is he doing here?*

"Greetings," she said, pressing the button on the monitor so he could hear her in the hallway.

"Greetings, Agent Kimba," he said, looking directly at the monitor on his side of the door. "I am sorry for my interruption to your rest time, but in the dining hall I overheard your desire to visit the forested room on the ship. You are correct. There are trees there just like the Christmas tree you are missing from your Earth home. Would you like to see them close-up?"

"Of course," she said, "but it is not part of my schedule. Mother and Father don't think it is a good idea."

"I see," Janus said. Then he cocked his head. "I won't tell if you won't. It would be a secret adventure, just between us agents."

Kimba hesitated on her side of the wall. Was this a way to get around the resistance her parents were putting up? What could it hurt to just take a tour of the forest room with another agent?

"Can you get me in there?" she finally asked.

"But of course." Janus swished his tail with pride. "All agents have access to the training rooms."

Kimba felt her fur prickle. She thought back on what Miss Fatty Cat had said before she'd transferred up to the ship—about her only job being to look pretty and do as she was told. That made the fur rise up all along her back in agitation. She was an agent. She should have access to all the rooms as well, not be treated like a baby who couldn't handle the same training as other agents.

She looked back at the monitor. Could she trust Janus? Mother had been very clear about not leaving her quarters without a guard of some kind.

"I should probably wait for Francis or Thoth before I leave my room," she admitted reluctantly.

"If you wish," Janus said. "But neither of those tomcats is going to allow you to visit the forest without your parents' permission. I, however, would be happy to escort you there immediately. We can apologize for your disobedience later."

Kimba pondered this, but she knew Janus was right. Father and Thoth had blocked her visits to the forest room at every turn. And Janus was an agent, after all.

What could be the danger in having him as a guard instead of Francis?

With a tap of her paw, the door slid open.

Janus sat up a bit straighter when he saw her, then he wrapped his tail around his front legs.

"Greetings, Agent Kimba," he said with a small nod of his head.

"Greetings, Agent Janus," she said and returned the nod.

"Right this way to the wilderness and predator training room."

Kimba glanced back into her quarters. Should she tell Thoth where she was going? No. He'd only try to stop her. Janus was right. If Mother found out, they could just say they were sorry.

She stepped out, shut the door behind her, and followed the two-toned cat through the maze of hallways in the ship. The few cats they passed along the way nodded politely or pretended to be involved in very important conversations and not to notice them at all.

When they arrived at the wilderness room, there was no guard on duty outside the large green door. Kimba sensed Janus was anxious, but maybe that was just because he was worried about getting in trouble with the high commander. He stalked up to the keypad next to the big doors, punched in a code, and stepped back as the doors swished apart to let them pass.

"After you," he said with a bow of his head.

Kimba stepped nimbly through the door and found herself on a platform high above the forest. Safety railings at three different heights kept her from feeling like she would fall right into the trees if she wasn't careful. To her right, there was a contraption with wheels and pulleys.

"This is one of the observation decks," Janus said. "The lift over there will take us down to the forest floor. Are you ready?"

Kimba gazed out over the tops of the trees. It smelled exactly like the forest outside her home in Arkansas, which was very odd inside the spaceship. The aromas and the view reminded her of sitting in an open window of their house atop the mountain. It also made her fur rise, remembering her long night hiding outside at the wildlife refuge. She could see a small stream in the distance, but even now that she was inside, she could not see the walls for the other three sides of the room. Her heart pitter-pattered at the very thought of venturing into all of that wildness.

Janus shifted his weight. "We don't have to go down there if you don't want to."

"No, no," Kimba sputtered. "I want to. It's just so huge. I've been lost in a forest kind of like this before. Seeing one again is just stirring up those memories. But there's nothing dangerous in this room, is there?" *No lions or tigers or bears?* she thought.

"Not right now," Janus assured her. "Unless a training session is going on, there are no animals in the room."

"Okay, then," Kimba said and headed over to the lift platform.

"Watch your step," Janus cautioned as they both hopped onto the lift.

Janus pressed a green button, and the platform lowered them down to the forest floor. Kimba trotted out and padded around a bit, enjoying the feel of the grass under her paws. It wasn't as sharp and pokey as the grass she remembered from her one time outside in Houston.

"Is this room really like an Earth forest?" Janus asked.

"Haven't you been to Earth?" Kimba said, surprised.

"Not yet," he admitted. "I've been through all of my training, but I haven't taken my first off-ship assignment yet."

"Oh. Well, yes. This is really what the forest is like, at least where I live on Earth. The Big Black Beast in my home actually spent a night out in the woods all by himself. He would be a better judge of it, I suppose. I know he met other beasts like him, and coyotes and a bear and a rattlesnake."

Kimba swallowed a lump in her throat at the thought that dangerous wild animals were ever in that room. She glanced around with widened pupils, but there was nothing there besides trees and rocks and the sound of the stream in the distance.

"So which one looks like the Christmas tree you are missing out on this year?" Janus asked.

Kimba trotted along a cleared space that created a path through the woods. There were all kinds of trees along the way, but none looked quite right. She had spotted a Christmassy tree from up high on the platform, so she kept looking. Finally, they rounded a corner and were face-to-face with a perfect cone-shaped fir tree.

"This one," she said. "This is what the Christmas tree in my house looks like. Except there is not so much trunk. "

"Interesting," Janus said as he walked around the base of the tree and looked it up and down.

"But the one in my house comes out of a box and is made of plastic and metal. The humans have to put it together."

"That's odd," Janus said. "Why don't they just cut one down from your forest and bring it in the house? It's a strange tradition altogether. Why does

114

there need to be a tree inside the house?"

"It's apparently something millions of humans do every year to celebrate the Christmas holiday. I suppose it's part of my job on Earth to learn about this kind of tradition. Miss Fluffernutter is putting together some historical research for me to study."

"Do they take turns climbing it?" he asked, sitting down next to her. "That would certainly add some fun and practicality to having a tree in the house."

"Oh no. Climbing it is not allowed. My sister and I got in trouble for doing that the first year we celebrated with our family. The humans decorate it with all kinds of fragile balls and bells and things that look like children's toys. Our tree has a mechanical light thing at the top that spins and shines different colors all over the room. Then they wrap presents for each other and put them underneath the tree. On Christmas day, the presents are opened, and then the tree is packed up and put away a few days later. Mama likes to have it done before the start of the new calendar year, but Daddy keeps it up in the living room as long as he can."

"Stranger and stranger," Janus said, gazing up to the top of the tree towering above them.

"The ones inside houses for Christmas are not nearly this big," she said. "They have to fit and not touch the ceiling. Maybe that's why my humans have a plastic one, so they're always sure to have a tree that is the right size."

"You can climb this one, you know," he said with a twinkle in his eye.

Kimba looked over at Janus, and his right ear swiveled back and forth, waiting for her to consider this possibility. She let her gaze run all the way up the tree, from the bottom to the top. At least as much of the top as she could see. It made her a bit dizzy to tip her head back that far.

"I climbed a fence one time," she admitted, "when I was trapped at the wildlife refuge, and I'm really good at climbing ladders, but I've never climbed a tree."

"Oh, it's easy. And it's one of the first lessons of the wildlife training room. The best way to escape a wild animal is to climb a tree to safety. As long as it's not an animal who can just climb after you, like a cougar or a bobcat."

"Well, if that's the first lesson, I suppose I should try," Kimba said with much more self-confidence than she really felt.

"Here," Janus said. "I'll show you. First you want to make sure your claws are ready. If you were on an outdoor mission, you'd want to do this every morning and evening to be sure you could climb in an emergency."

He turned to a nearby log and ripped at it with his front claws. Kimba saw a couple of sheaths from his nails fly through the air and land in the grass nearby. Sharpening claws was something she already knew how to do, so she joined him at the log, ripping and tearing at it and losing a few sheaths of her own in the process. Then they both climbed on top of the log and scratched with their back claws.

When Janus was satisfied that his claws had been cleaned and were ready, he hopped down and sauntered over to the tree. Leaping up, he grabbed around the trunk with all four paws and dug in his claws. Then he worked his way up to the first large branch, using his claws to hop-pull himself along. He settled on the branch, looking down at Kimba.

"Now you try. You just need to get up to here. A tree like this with so many branches is an easy climb."

Even though her heart felt like it was beating in her throat, Kimba jumped off the log and trotted over to the tree. She looked up at Janus.

"You can do it," he said encouragingly. "Just jump and start climbing. Don't think about it too much. Cats are climbers. Your instinct will kick in once you start."

Kimba took a deep breath and hoped he was right. Then she leaped and hugged the tree like she had seen Janus do. Up and up, she dragged/hopped herself along until she reached the branch where Janus sat waiting. With a final pull, she sat down next to him and dug in her claws to hang on.

"Excellent!" he said. "How'd it feel?"

"Amazing," Kimba whispered. "Exhilarating!" Her heart was still pounding, but the first rush of fear had passed.

"Ready to go higher?"

"Absolutely!"

Janus twitched his whiskers in amusement at her enthusiasm and started to work his way up to the next branch. He just hoped Commander Horus had set her side of things in motion.

Getting Kimba up a tree was only the first step of the plan.

13

WHERE'S KIMBA?

Francis scratched on the door again. What could Kimba be doing that she couldn't hear it? Was she sleeping so soundly she didn't notice? Had Thoth already picked her up and taken her to the next event on the schedule? Surely he would have notified someone of that.

Francis hit the buzzer on the intercom and waited a full minute. Still nothing.

Out of the corner of his eye, Francis spotted Thoth trotting down the hall toward him. The tortie cat was alone. A chill ran along Francis's spine and raised his hackles.

"Greetings, Francis," Thoth said cheerily. "Is Kimba still asleep?"

"Greetings, Agent Thoth. I have been scratching for several minutes and even used the buzzer. Agent Kimba is not answering."

"That's odd. She couldn't have slept through the buzzer." He stepped up to the intercom and pressed the speaker button. "Kimba? Is everything okay in there?"

The two cats waited anxiously, but there was still no response.

"Do you know the override code for this guest room?" Thoth finally asked, his pupils wide, eyes dark and worried.

"Of course. It is the same for all of the guest rooms, but I really ought to speak with the high commander before invading Kimba's quarters."

"What if something is wrong? Do you want to wait for an answer?"

Francis considered that and then punched a six-digit code into the keypad. The guest room doors swished open to each side, and they peeked in.

"Kimba?" Thoth called out.

Francis stalked around the room, tail held high. Then he locked eyes with Thoth.

"She is not here. Could she have left with the high commander?"

Thoth glanced over at the computer monitor and noticed that the red button was lit up. Probably from the message he had sent her a few minutes earlier to see if she was awake, but it could also be from the high commander. Not wanting to listen to Kimba's private messages, Thoth typed in a call to High Commander Felicity directly. He was quickly greeted by the face of a sleek black cat.

"One moment please, Agent Kimba."

The cat had clearly not looked in the monitor but had just noted what room the transmission was coming from. Thoth waited impatiently, his ears laid back. After a long thirty seconds, Felicity's face appeared.

"Greetings, My Daughter." Then she hesitated, seeing Thoth's anxious face instead of Kimba's. "Agent Thoth? Why are you contacting me from this device? Is everything okay?"

"I'm not sure," Thoth admitted. "Kimba clearly isn't with you."

"No, she's not." Felicity sat up taller and felt her tail puff. "And she's obviously not with you. Her father is here, so she's not with him either. Where is Francis?"

"I am here, High Commander," Francis said, walking up behind Thoth so she could see him. "Please excuse my forwardness in entering your daughter's room without permission, but after an extended period of trying to rouse her, Agent Thoth and I feared she might be ill or injured."

"That is certainly acceptable reasoning, Francis. Think nothing of it. But please update me as to Kimba's status."

"I'm afraid I cannot," Francis said, his whiskers dropping. "She is not here."

"Her room is empty," Thoth confirmed. "It sounds like she didn't contact any of us about where she went."

"She clearly did not," Felicity said, attempting to control her temper—and her fears.

"There is no sign of a struggle or any unhappy event," Francis assured her.

Thoth laid his ears back again. Danger like that had not occurred to him as it logically would to a guard like Francis. He looked around the room himself. No. No signs of anything bad having happened.

Felicity typed for a few seconds and then sighed.

"The protective shield is still in place around her guest quarters. No one could have transferred her out."

Thoth swallowed around the lump in his throat. That hadn't crossed his mind either, and he knew it should have.

"She must have left of her own volition," Francis concluded.

"But where in the world would she go without someone to accompany her?" Felicity demanded. "She would get lost just trying to find the dining hall for a snack."

Thoth and Francis looked at each other, but neither one of them had an answer.

"Agent Bennett!" Felicity called over her shoulder.

Thoth saw the sleek black cat come into view behind the high commander.

"Start a search of every security camera on the ship. We must locate Agent Kimba *immediately*."

Bennett nodded and hurried off to another computer station across the room.

Thoth sat down on one of the cushions in Kimba's room with a frustrated flump. Where in the world would Kimba have gone all by herself?

14

UP A TREE

Kimba was stuck. Seriously stuck. She had run into a V in the pine tree, where the branches forked off in two different directions. In her excitement to get higher, she hadn't thought it all through and planned her route. Now she had her back paws on one branch and her front paws on another with her belly suspended in the air between them. Hanging on desperately with her claws, she wasn't sure if it was better to push off onto the branch or try to get back to the trunk.

"Jump to the branch!" Janus called to her from

higher up in the tree.

She could hear the laughter in his voice and it made her fur rankle, though she did as he said. Pushing off firmly with her back feet, she tried for the branch but ended up hanging with her back legs dangling. With much scrambling and hissing, she finally got on top of it. But as she hunkered on the branch to rest, she also looked down.

All

The

Way

Down.

Her stomach flipped, and it felt like the tree was spinning. Or maybe it was the ground that was spinning. Whatever it was, she was pretty sure it was going to make her fall. She dug in her claws and clung to the branch with all her might.

"Did you look down?" Janus asked.

Kimba couldn't put the words together in her head to answer.

Janus quickly scampered down the tree—hind end first, like a confused squirrel—and stopped on a branch across from her. She looked at him with panicked eyes.

"It probably won't help if I tell you this happens to pretty much every cat during their first climb," he said.

Kimba shook her head no. That didn't help at all.

"You aren't really all that high," he assured her. "If you fell from here, you'd be okay."

She looked through the maze of branches she could bang into along the way to the bottom and didn't think that was true at all.

"We can just hang out here until you get your bearings a bit," he said. "Then we can keep going or head back down."

"Okay," she mumbled, wondering how long getting her bearings would take.

A loud crash, like a tree falling, came from somewhere in the distance.

"Oh no," Janus said. "Someone must be starting a training session."

"What?!" Kimba gasped.

"Ssshhh. If we just sit tight, they will never even

know we are here. I didn't log us in. There's no way you could get in trouble."

Whatever training session was starting, she and Janus were going to be in the middle of it.

No one knows where I am! Kimba thought with horror.

It suddenly occurred to her that this whole adventure had been a horribly terrible idea.

"I've found her," Agent Bennett called out across headquarters. "Or at least we can see when she left her quarters."

Thoth, Francis, and the high commander raced across the room toward him.

"Show us," Felicity said.

Bennett pulled up the footage from the intercom system on Kimba's guest quarters and played it for them. Thoth's eyes narrowed as they listened to the conversation.

"That's Agent Janus," he said.

His whiskers stiffened as he remembered passing

Janus in the hall when Kimba first arrived. She had already known who he was then. Thoth struggled with his feelings about that. Was he worried for Kimba's safety or just jealous?

"Who is this Agent Janus?" Felicity demanded. "And how does Kimba know him well enough to trust him like this?"

"I do not know, High Commander," Francis said. "But at least we know where she was headed an hour ago."

"She asked about Agent Janus and his unique coloring when we passed him earlier," Thoth admitted, "but I didn't realize she knew him that well."

Felicity looked back at the screen, where it showed Kimba walking off down the hallway with Janus. As they were all considering their next steps, Commander Griffin arrived in a huff of fur and whiskers.

"Where is she?!" he yelled. "Have you found her?"

"Calm yourself, Griffin," Felicity said. "All seems to be well."

She motioned to the screen, and Griffin considered it for a moment.

"Who is that she's with?" he asked his mate.

"His name is Agent Janus, but I don't know more about him yet."

"An agent?"

"Well, an agent for now," Felicity said with a twitch of her whiskers.

"And what does this Janus think he's up to, taking her from her room without a guard?"

"From what we hear on the recording, he's taking her to the wilderness training room."

Griffin sat down with a plop, and the others stared at him.

"But I told her she couldn't go there," he said.

"As did I," Felicity said.

Thoth didn't realize how many times Kimba had asked to visit that room. Apparently, she had taken matters into her own paws.

"There they are," Bennett said, pulling up security video from outside the wilderness training room.

"You can see them both going inside through the main doors, though they didn't sign in like they should have."

"Well, at least we know where she was not too long ago," Felicity said. "We can go collect them and have a chat with this Agent Janus."

"High commander," Bennett said with trepidation, "there's something else."

"Yes? What is it?"

"The schedule shows a last-minute training session is planned for this time period. It has already started."

"What kind of training session?" Griffin asked.

Bennett, his eyes dark and wide, glanced over at Thoth and then at Francis. The guard glared at him.

"Cough it up," Francis said.

"It is an aggressive animal forest escape training, already in progress. I've confirmed the transfer of a creature from Earth to the ship."

"Is Kimba still in the room?" Felicity asked.

Bennett nodded his head slowly. "I fear so. No camera recorded her leaving."

"What kind of creature?" Thoth asked, his hackles spiking at the thought of his Kimba in a forest, even a pretend one, with a wild animal.

The whole group stared at Bennett expectantly. He tapped a key and brought up an image of the animal on the screen.

Felicity took two steps back and tried not to faint as the seriousness of the situation hit her.

"Francis, would you please get my youngest daughter out of there as quickly as possible."

15
MONSTER IN THE ROOM

A low grumble echoed through the forest. Every hair on Kimba's body stood on end, and her ears and nose flushed red.

"What was that?"

"I don't know," Janus answered honestly.

He knew the basic plan, but Commander Horus had not shared with him what animal would be turned loose in the training room. From the sounds the creature was making, it was a very large animal. A *very annoyed*, very large animal. And Janus was now supposed to rescue Kimba and gain her trust

—and maybe the trust of the high command as well—to help further the plans of the League for Cat Equality. He flexed his claws in and out on the branch where he sat.

"We are safe here in the tree for now," he whispered to Kimba. "Even if it is an animal that can climb, if we stay quiet, it shouldn't notice us."

"But if we run, couldn't we make it back to the entrance and the lift out before it gets here?"

"How fast do you think you can climb down?"

Kimba looked at the ground and felt her head swim again. The idea of climbing down at all—slowly or quickly—was terrifying.

"Stay here," he said. "I'm going to climb higher and try to see what's going on."

Pine needles rained down on her as Janus scrambled up the tree.

What was I thinking, sneaking off to climb Christmas trees? Maybe Mother and Father were totally right and I have no business being in this room for even one minute. What if the beast catches me and eats me, fur and all, and leaves nothing behind, and

I'm dead, and no one but Janus ever knows where I ended up? Will he be too afraid to admit what happened?

Her heart was racing so fast, she started panting. It took her full focus to hang onto the branch and not drool in panic.

"Kimba," Janus whisper-called down to her, "don't move or make a sound. Be perfectly still."

Kimba froze.

Below the tree, she heard the snap of a twig and the huffing and puffing of whatever animal had been transferred in with them. Something about those sounds and the smell of the creature was familiar. Curiosity got the best of her, and she tipped her head just enough to look down the tree.

Through the branches, she could see the brown furry shape of the animal. Its head came into view as it snuffled up and down the tree trunk.

It can smell me! Can it climb a tree?

One brown eye came into view below her. Then another. After more grumbling and huffing from the creature, it started violently rubbing against the tree.

"Hang on!" Janus yelled.

And she did, with all four sets of claws. The trunk wasn't very thick, and she clung to the branch as the whole tree swayed and rocked back and forth against the animal's weight. When the motion finally stopped, Kimba glanced back down again.

A furry brown face stared right at her.

Dark-brown eyes met hers.

Then she realized why the smell was so familiar. She recognized the round ears and long snout and the snuffing noises. She had met one of these animals before.

It was a massive grizzly bear.

"It's okay," she called up to Janus. "It's a bear. I can explain to him what is happening and that we won't bother him."

"What? You can't talk to a bear!" Janus said, ears laid back flat.

"Of course you can."

"What in the universe do you know about talking to bears?"

"Well," Kimba said, "I've done it before. Why should this bear be any different?"

Janus stared at her, the fur on his whole body a-puff.

"You've talked to a bear?"

"Absolutely. When those nasty rebels stranded me at the wildlife refuge. I think his name was Bam Bam. He was very nice."

Of course, there were thick metal bars between us then.

She wondered if wild bears were the same. There was only one way to test her theory.

"Hello, down there!" she called out.

The bear tipped his head, but he didn't answer.

"I know this is all strange," Kimba said, "and you are probably terribly confused, but everything is really just fine. There's nothing to be upset about."

The bear either didn't understand or he didn't agree at all. His eyes glared at her in fury, and he directed several angry snorts up the trunk of the tree.

"Hufff. Hufff. Hufff."

Kimba wasn't sure if she should try saying something calming, but the creature answered that question quickly. He thrashed his massive head back and forth, stomping his front feet from side to side.

Then he roared—the most horrifying sound Kimba had ever heard. That roar filled the forest and swept up the tree as the grizzly bared his fangs at her. Every hair on her body stood straight up again as the smell of his breath washed over her.

Maybe she couldn't talk to this bear. She wondered if she had made another horribly terrible mistake.

With a snarl, the bear leapt his front legs up on the trunk of the tree. He shoved it over and over and over and over, shaking the trunk even more violently than before. Kimba heard Janus yell something, but her ears were still ringing from the roar. She clung to the branch like her life depended on it—because it actually did. But no matter how fiercely she gripped the branch, the shuddering and swaying of the grizzly's attack was too much.

Her back paws slipped. Clinging by only her

front paws, Kimba dangled from the branch and thrashed desperately with her back feet for something to hold on to. The trunk was too far away, but she gasped and clawed at it anyway.

What am I doing here? What am I doing here? What am I doing here? raced round and round in her mind. She couldn't hold on like that for much longer.

Finally, the shaking stopped and she managed to brace her back legs tentatively on another branch and look down at the bear again. He was still on the attack and started shouldering his way through the first few layers of branches, ripping them from his path and snapping them like twigs. Kimba watched in horror as his thick, razor-sharp claws ripped at the bark and the terrifying jaws grew closer and closer. She debated climbing higher, but her paws wouldn't move.

"We are not food!" Janus howled at the creature.

How far up can the bear climb? she wondered.

The tree swayed and rocked as the grizzly tore at the trunk in his efforts to reach her. In a panic, she could only think of one thing to do.

"Stop that right now!" she yelled down at the bear. An instinctive hiss tore at her throat. "Hhhhkkk!"

Surprisingly, the bear stopped. Maybe he'd never been hissed at before. He scowled up at her, his head only a few feet away now that he was standing up along the trunk.

"What you doing in my forest?" he growled. "Why my forest smell bad?"

Kimba panted to catch her breath.

"I'm sorry to have to tell you," she said with a gasp, "but this isn't your forest. You have been . . ." Explaining about a spaceship full of cats seemed too complicated and probably too much for a wild bear to understand. "You have been moved to another forest."

"Moved?" he asked. "How moved?"

"It's hard to explain, but it's only for a little while. It's temporary. You will be returned home soon, and everything will go back to normal." *At least that's how I think it works.*

"Go home soon?" he asked with a whine. "To my forest?"

"Yes," Kimba promised. "Very soon. But you have to behave yourself until then."

The bear seemed to ponder this, then he pushed off the trunk with his front legs and landed with a thud, all four paws back on the ground.

Kimba gathered up every ounce of courage she had and started to work her way down the tree—back legs first, like she had seen Janus do. It was truly the most terrifying thing she had ever done because she couldn't keep an eye on the bear and climb down at the same time. What if he changed his mind and came after her again?

I hope he understood that "not food" part.

When she stopped on a broken branch in the middle of the creature's destruction, she noticed the bear was just sitting underneath her. His back legs stuck out awkwardly to one side, and he was sniffing the air around him. Pine needles hit Kimba on the head, and she looked up to see Janus coming down the tree toward her.

"Wait," she whispered. "I don't think he has seen you yet."

Janus stopped where he was, but his ears twisted

and his whiskers twitched in frustration.

"Mr. Bear," Kimba said, "did you run into any other cats in this strange forest?"

The bear swung his head slowly from side to side.

"No little cats like you," he said. "My forest has cats, but they are big and fierce. I stay away from them." He looked up at Kimba, his long face droopy and sad. "You are tiny, like little bird."

Kimba wondered where the other cats were. If the bear had been transferred in for a training session, wouldn't there be at least one other cat around somewhere? Some agent should be trying to escape from him. Someone should be watching, shouldn't they? She wasn't sure if she should come out of the tree so the cats in charge could see her or stay hidden. It might still be possible to sneak out without her parents ever discovering she had been in the forbidden room.

"Oh," the bear said. "My toes feel funny."

He looked back up at Kimba, about ready to say something else. There was a flash of light, and he was gone.

Kimba heard Janus sigh, and pine needles rained

on her and stuck in her white fur as he scrambled to her branch.

"Are you okay?" he asked as he settled in next to her.

"Sure," she said. "I think he was mostly just scared and confused. I hope he's safe now. It seems risky to transfer an animal that doesn't understand the process. Doesn't that sort of break the main rule for transfers?"

Janus shrugged. "It's just a bear." He licked his front paw three times and then wiped it across his face. "Ugh. The sap from this tree is so sticky. It's going to take hours of grooming to get it all off. No wonder we don't usually climb fir trees."

"But what if something goes wrong?" she asked.

He paused, his tongue sticking out of his mouth a tiny bit. "What would go wrong with my grooming?"

"No, with the bear. What if he gets hurt because he doesn't understand about transfers?"

"Earth will certainly survive without one bear."

Kimba felt her ears flush pink. She was about to

argue that every animal was valuable and that risking a bear's life was cruel, but a loud clang from somewhere in the forest interrupted her.

"Sounds like our fun is over," Janus said.

"Do they know we're here?"

"Well, someone removed the bear. It wasn't nearly enough time for any training session to be over."

Kimba heard voices coming closer. Then a massive gray face looked up at her through the tree branches. Not as big as the bear's, but it was big enough. And very, very angry.

"Greetings, Francis," she said with a sigh.

"The high commander is waiting for you in her quarters," Francis said. "Can you climb down on your own?"

Without answering, Kimba slunk down the rest of the way until her paws were on the ground again. She tried to shake off the pine needles, but most of them stuck to her fur like they were glued there.

"I will give you a few minutes to tidy yourself," Francis said. "You can't possibly walk through the halls of the ship like that."

Kimba sighed and got to work. The sap from the tree was bitter, and she wondered if she would ever get it all out of her fur. Maybe she should visit the grooming salon and get some help.

Francis shifted his attention back up the tree.

"Agent Janus, Commander Griffin is waiting to speak with you *privately*."

Janus backed down the tree slowly. Once he was on the ground again, he began to pull the pine needles from his fur.

"No need to bother with that right now," Francis said. "Commander Griffin is waiting for you in the viewing room at the corner of the forest."

Janus sighed and then lifted his head proudly.

"Agent Kimba," he said, "I hope your experience in the wilderness training room was everything you'd hoped for."

Francis glared at him, but Janus merely lifted his tail and stalked toward the corner of the room, where Commander Griffin was waiting.

Kimba watched him leave. She could not imagine exactly what reprimand her father might give him, but she suspected it wouldn't be any fun for Janus.

"Please express some urgency," Francis said to her. "It is not polite to keep the high commander waiting."

"Sorry," she murmured as she resumed picking the sap and needles from her fur.

"It's too bad the bear chased you up a pine tree. Very tricky to deal with."

"Oh, he didn't chase us up there. This is the tree I wanted to climb."

Francis looked at her like she had lost her mind. "Whatever for?"

Realizing how silly her logic would seem to a ship cat like Francis, Kimba almost didn't answer, but she knew he wanted some explanation.

"Because it looks like the Christmas tree at home," she said quietly.

"I see," he said with a flick of his whiskers.

But she was positive he did not.

16

APOLOGIES AND AFTERMATH

Kimba sat quietly and respectfully while the high commander dished out a tirade of scolding. On Earth, Mama had been upset with her now and then for silly things. Even for trying to climb the plastic and metal Christmas tree. But that reprimand usually was nothing more than a "No!" and some shushing noises to scare her away from the object in question. High Commander Felicity had much more than "No" to say about Kimba's adventure in the wilderness room. Kimba was pretty sure it would be time for a shift change on the ship before her mother finished with everything she had to say on the subject.

"And what if we hadn't found you in time?" the high commander said, not waiting for an answer. "That bear could have bitten you in two without a thought."

Her mother paused and stared at her. Maybe she really did want some response.

"I understand it was wrong to sneak off," Kimba said, "but there was never supposed to be any danger. Janus was just going to let me see the room and climb a tree. There wasn't supposed to be an animal in there or a training session going on."

"There *was not* a training session going on," her mother said, her whiskers stiff with anger.

"Then where did the bear come from?"

Felicity stared at her daughter, letting her ponder that part through for herself.

It didn't take Kimba long. Her ears flushed deep red.

"Someone put the bear in the wilderness room because they knew I was in there."

"And there it is," her mother said. "You ran off without any protection, and you were nearly killed. Again!"

"The bear wasn't going to kill me. I had already calmed it down before it was transferred back out."

"That's not the point. The creature was *supposed* to kill you. Or scare or hurt you at the very least. You walked right into a trap!"

Kimba let that sink in too.

"Janus tricked me?"

"We are not certain of that yet," Felicity admitted. "Your father is sorting out that side of things. The rebels could have just been following you and taken advantage of your carelessness and disobedience. But you are to have no further contact with Agent Janus, just in case."

Kimba didn't envy Janus his conversation with Commander Griffin, but not seeing him again wasn't a problem. She barely knew him. She lowered her head and nodded respectfully, to show the high commander she understood.

"It is nearly time for you to return to your Earth

home," her mother said more calmly. "I'll have some food sent to your room, and then why don't you get some sleep. We have one final event scheduled before you leave."

"Yes, Mother." Sleep sounded like a fantastic idea.

"And don't leave your quarters again without a guard."

"Yes, Mother."

"A *bear*! Seriously?" Janus paced back and forth in the small, dark room. "You put a bear in there with us!"

Rebel Commander Horus chuckled and licked her front paw.

"Would you have preferred a coyote?" Horus asked.

"Of course not. I was thinking it would be something more like a skunk or a badger. No real danger."

Horus flipped her fluffy tail and then wrapped it around her body.

"None of that matters now. Kimba is safe and

back in the clutches of her parents. She will leave the ship shortly. And none of this can be traced to you or to me."

"Are you positive? Commander Griffin has forbidden me to come anywhere near Kimba again. How am I supposed to continue to turn her to our side if I can't even see her?"

"She will be back on the ship permanently soon enough. And you have just become something most interesting to a young and strong-willed cat like Kimba. You are *forbidden*. Saying something is off-limits makes a cat want it twice as much."

"I hope you're right," Janus said. "I didn't really get to save her like we planned, but we did share a unique experience."

"Trust me. You and Kimba are only at the beginning of your lives. There is plenty of time for our plans to unfold. The League for Cat Equality is not going anywhere. Just be patient and watch for signs of her next visit."

Kimba slept for so long, she found it hard to wake up and move again. Every muscle in her body was sore, right to the tip of her tail. For a house cat who never does much of anything, a wild day of climbing and fright had left her exhausted. She stretched and worked out the kinks from her legs.

After some grooming, Kimba pressed the communication button to let her mother know she was awake. It had certainly been an intense visit—much more interesting than any Christmas she'd ever had on Earth. There had definitely been a tree involved. No presents, though.

A few minutes later, the buzzer on her door sounded. Kimba pressed the monitor and saw Thoth sitting in the hallway. She hadn't spoken with him since the wilderness room fiasco.

"Greetings, Agent Thoth," she said into the speaker.

"Greetings, Agent Kimba," he answered formally from his side. "You indicated that you are ready for your last scheduled event before your return to Earth."

She pressed the button to open the door and

153

found herself face-to-face with a very stern Thoth —ears tall and whiskers pursed—looking like someone had rubbed all of his fur the wrong way.

"I'm sorry," she said, eyes cast down. "I can see you're mad at me too for running off and not following the rules."

He relaxed a bit, trying to adjust his body language.

"I'm not angry, really," he said. "But I certainly did not enjoy watching a bear try to tear you out of a tree, knowing there was nothing I could do about it."

"You saw that?"

"There are observation monitors everywhere. That's how we found you in the first place."

"Then I'm sorry I worried you."

"All's well that ends well, as the humans like to say. But it would be nice not to have to rescue you again anytime soon."

Kimba stepped out into the hall and shut the door behind her.

"Well, I don't know that anyone *rescued* me," she

said. "By the time the bear was transferred away, I had already calmed him down and was totally safe."

"Fine. I didn't rescue you. But maybe we could have less drama and fewer wild animals in your life for a while. No bears. No tigers. Or ligers. Or angry beasts chasing you around apartments on Earth."

She nodded and followed him down the bright-white hallway.

"My Earth life is really boring and quiet," she said. "It's only when I get involved with ship stuff that danger seems to be around every corner."

"That's part of being an agent, but it was not supposed to be a part of this trip."

"No, I guess not. I managed to find that excitement all by myself."

"With a little help from Agent Janus," Thoth added.

Kimba glanced his way, not sure how to respond to that part. *Has Mother found a connection between Janus and the rebels?*

"He just helped me get into the room," she said. "It was my idea."

"Maybe you should listen to the advice of cats you know you can trust instead of running off with strangers," he said with a flick of his tail.

Going off with Janus seems to have made him angrier than the fact that I went into the training room, she thought. She didn't understand why that should be such a big deal. Janus was another agent, after all.

"I just hope," he said, "the next time your parents say no to you, that you listen."

Kimba rankled at being told what to do, but part of her knew he was right. She understood very little about life on the ship. It was probably safer to follow the rules and be obedient. At least for now.

They trotted down the hall in silence for several minutes. Then Thoth stopped at a lift and pressed some buttons.

"We will have to go down two levels," he said.

Kimba felt her toes tingle as the lift arrived and vibrated the floor around her. A door slid open and revealed a room about the size of a closet. Thoth headed right in, but Kimba held back a second. She'd never been in an enclosed lift like that. All her tours around the ship had been on the same level. Not wanting to seem like a fraidy-cat, she skittered inside and sat down, but her heart was racing.

Thoth punched a button, and the door closed with a swish. Then it felt like the floor dropped out beneath her. Kimba tried to dig her claws into the tile, and they made a little screeching noise. Thoth glanced at her, so she did her best to look calm and in control. He probably rode lifts on the ship all the time, since he was a kitten, and would find her fear silly. Before he could say anything, the lift vibrated to a stop and the door swished open again.

"Here we are," he said. "The Great Hall is just down this way."

Kimba peeked out the door and saw nothing but more white hallways, like every other part of the ship.

"Follow me," Thoth said. "I hope you like the surprise we have planned for you."

17
MERRY CHRISTMAS

Thoth held back and let Kimba enter the Great Hall first. She stepped through the gigantic door and froze. The Great Hall served its name well. It was as massive and sprawling as headquarters, but the ceiling was vaulted high. It was white and cheery where headquarters was dark and somber. Kimba's back legs felt limp beneath her, but she managed to stay standing. The scene was beyond belief.

Every inch of the room was covered with Christmas. There were dozens of huge evergreen trees, decorated with a variety of ornaments and garlands. Tables around the room were covered with festive treats. They looked like the normal bits of fish or mouse served on the ship, but red and green tufts of decoration surrounded them. Hundreds of cats wandered here and there, putting finishing touches on the displays.

She turned to face Thoth, who hovered behind her.

"Who did this?" she asked in wonder.

"I did," he said, "with some help. I read the documents you asked Miss Fluffernutter to gather about the holiday because I felt like you were really missing Christmas with your sister and Earth family."

"You did this for me?"

"I thought maybe we could celebrate in some simple way here on the ship. But the more I read about it, the more different ways of honoring the holiday I discovered. Many people on Earth don't celebrate Christmas at all."

"Really?" she said. "I thought every family was like my humans."

"We are always surprised at how varied humans are around the planet. That's why we have to employ so many agents. Even within the same continent, humans have so many ways of thinking and behaving. It is quite confusing. And they change from century to century. Not like cats at all."

High Commander Felicity stepped down from a platform at the side of the room and strode toward the pair at the door.

"Don't hesitate, My Daughter. Many agents have worked hard to create this party for you."

"It's amazing!" Kimba said as she moved slowly into the room.

Everywhere she looked there were colors and sparkling objects and dangling things to tempt her. It was like Christmas in her Earth home, just ten times bigger.

"The transfer platform has been busy," Thoth said with a proud swish of his tail.

"You brought all this up from the planet with transfers?"

The high commander nodded her head and glanced at Thoth.

"Agent Thoth scanned the houses around North America and found bits and pieces that could be transferred up and sent to this room. We are borrowing some decorations while it is nighttime on Earth and their celebrating is done. Once our party is over, we can simply return them where they belong."

Thoth flicked his tail at the word "simply." It was going to be a major undertaking to get every tree and wreath back to the correct home in one piece, but he would do anything to make Kimba happy. From the look on her face, he had been successful. Her eyes were wide and sparkling in the red and green lights of the room.

Her mother stepped over to a fully decorated evergreen tree nearby that looked familiar.

"Is that the tree from my house?" Kimba said with a gasp.

"It is," Felicity said. "We knew it was safe to transfer this one because there are no humans in the house to miss it. It would also be special to you."

"Yes. It is very special." Kimba looked the tree up and down and felt a little clench in her stomach. It was strange to be away from her Earth family during the holiday.

Her mother sat down next to a gift with red-and-green striped paper and a huge red bow under the tree.

"As we understand it," Felicity said, "gifts are a part of the holiday."

Kimba nodded. "The humans buy each other things and wrap them up so it is a surprise."

"This one is for you, from your father and me."

Kimba trotted over to the gift and sniffed at it. Whatever it was, it was huge. Each side was wider than she was long.

"Open it," Thoth encouraged her.

Kimba used her front claws to rip through the wrapping paper and discovered an enormous fuzzy purple pillow inside. She wanted to climb right on top of it, nestle down, and take a long nap.

"This will be the first piece of furniture for your permanent room here on the ship," her mother said. "It is time for you to stop sleeping in visitor quarters. Your father and I have set aside a room near ours for you."

"My own room?" Kimba said in awe.

Part of her was excited. She'd never had a room all her own before. Everything in the human house belonged to Mama and Daddy. She had pillows that were sort of hers, but other cats could sleep there just as easily as she could. Nothing was 100% hers.

But another part of her realized that having her own quarters on the ship was one step closer to having the ship be her home. No more Earth. No more Mama or Daddy or Leia or Mindy. Maybe even no more Hiro for many years.

Thoth sensed her hesitation but didn't understand what was worrying her. It couldn't be the pillow. Every cat loves a big fluffy pillow. He had helped to select the present when the high commander told him about giving Kimba her own room. Maybe he'd just gotten the color wrong.

"Do you like purple?" he asked.

"Oh, yes, purple is lovely," she said, perking up her ears. "The gift is wonderful. I truly love it."

She bent over and rubbed the side of her face along the edge of the pillow, carefully marking it with her scent and a streak of white fur.

"I will have it taken to your new room immediately," the high commander said. "You can enjoy sleeping there tonight before you return to Earth."

She motioned to two nearby cats, and they immediately moved in to handle the pillow.

"Be sure she gets the bow as well," Thoth whispered to them. "That looks like it would be quite fun to shred."

Kimba looked around the room again. It was all quite breathtaking. She glanced back at Thoth.

"Thank you," she whispered. "I know this must have been a huge project for you."

"It's nothing," he said, struggling to keep his tail from puffing or thrashing in excitement.

Thoth knew Kimba would be heading back to the planet soon. It might be a year or more before he saw her in person again. He was glad she would have a happy memory that was attached to him to carry with her.

Miss Fluffernutter cleared her throat from across the room and caught their attention.

"Ah, yes," Felicity said. "The kittens have prepared a special performance for you."

Kimba trotted over to the tiara-wearing cat and noticed that today Miss Fluffernutter's tutu was a dazzling green. Her claws had even been painted red for the occasion. A group of two dozen or more puffy kittens were gathered around a particularly large Christmas tree. The kittens were fascinated by the trees and the ornaments, and they uttered adorable little squeaks and mews as their wide eyes took in the room around them.

"Greetings, Agent Kimba," Miss Fluffernutter said formally. "We did some research and learned a traditional Earth holiday carol to share with you."

She turned to the wiggling group of kittens and raised her front leg. They stilled as much as they could and locked their eyes on her. With a wave of her paw, the group began a rendition of "Silent Night" as only a chorus of kittens could.

Kimba recognized the song immediately. It was one Mama played over and over during December. It didn't sound quite the same sung by enthusiastic kittens, but it still made her fur tingle.

"Sleeeeeeep in heavenly pee-eeace. Sleee-eeep in heavenly peace," they mewed.

Kimba knew that humans clap at the end of a performance. She'd seen it on TV. But she wasn't sure what ship cats do to express praise. She looked to her mother. The high commander only nodded at the group of kittens. Kimba followed her mother's example and nodded at them as well, her eyes wide and bright.

"Excellent job," Felicity said. "I can see that you all practiced very diligently for that performance."

"Yes," Kimba added, "it was perfectly wonderful."

The compliments made the kittens squiggle and roll on their backs and squirm, and tiny purrs vibrated up from the group.

"Thank you, Miss Fluffernutter," Felicity continued. "As always, you present our future agents in their very best light."

Miss Fluffernutter bowed her tiara-crowned head to the high commander. Then she raised herself up tall, ears alert, and called the kittens back to order.

"Fall in line and follow me," she said.

To Kimba's amazement, the kittens did just that. Miss Fluffernutter high-stepped from the Great

Hall, tutu waggling and fluffy tail waving like a flag. Each little kitten fell into step behind her. Balls of fur in black and white and tawny and gray and orange and striped and even a couple of multi-colored calicos all pranced in a line behind their teacher.

"Thank you!" Kimba called after them.

Thoth stepped up beside her.

"There's one more thing we thought you might like," he said.

Thoth led her to a corner of the room, where a computer monitor was set up. He clicked a button, and the screen lit up an image. She squinted to see what it was, but then her pupils widened and her ears flushed pink.

Kimba could see Mama and Daddy and Leia and several other humans she recognized from when they had visited her Earth home. They were in a house she did not recognize, and they were all gathered around a Christmas tree with gifts and treats and lots of smiles.

"We recorded this earlier today," Thoth said. "I traced your fur registration on the human female, and we found them in this house in Michigan.

There's a large mirror in the living room, so we were able to see all of their holiday activities. It looks like they had a lovely Christmas Day."

"Yes, yes, it does," Kimba agreed.

"And here too," he said as he clicked another button. "We were able to tap in through the TV in the living room."

The screen split in two to include images coming from Mindy's apartment. There was a little tree there, tucked into a corner, and Kimba could see the girl and her cat, Slinky, curled up on the sofa. There was a beast sprawled out with them as well, probably the one Hiro said had visited with Mindy. Piles of wrapping paper were strewn around the room. They all looked happy and content. Kimba sighed.

Mindy must be missing her family at the holidays, she thought. *It must be hard to grow up and move away from home.*

She had been so busy on the ship, she hadn't thought about home too much, but seeing all of her favorite humans made her stomach ache a bit. Earth was still home, and she was happy to be going back there soon. Someday she would have to grow up and come back to the ship, probably forever. She knew that. But not just yet.

"Thank you, Thoth. This is all so amazing."

He blinked slowly at her and then turned to the high commander.

"Are the agents ready to make their presentations?" he asked her.

"Yes," she said. "And then the party can begin."

18
CHRISTMAS AROUND EARTH

The middle of the Great Hall was filled with decorated trees and tables of food, but Thoth led Kimba around to the tables placed along one wall of the room. Stopping at the first one, Kimba was met by a huge black-and-white cat wearing a Santa Claus hat. He looked uncomfortable with the strange red hat strapped to his head—and he looked rather like her father.

"I'm sure you remember your uncle, Special Agent Buddy," Thoth said.

"Retired agent," Buddy added. "Only for my niece

Kimba would I wear this silly hat."

"Greetings, Uncle Buddy," Kimba said happily. "You look very festive."

"Ho, ho, ho!" Buddy yowled.

Kimba tipped her head and pursed her whiskers in delight. On Buddy's table, there was a round centerpiece of evergreen branches with a red candle in the middle. There was also a set of little statues around a barn, like what Mama put out at their house during the holidays. But in the set at home, the figures were all cats.

Buddy cleared his throat before beginning his speech.

"In my studies of the families of North America who celebrate Christmas, most of them used these figures to represent the characters from the story of the birth of Jesus of Nazareth in the Bible. He's the baby there in the little box called a manger. His birth would apparently have taken place at another time and season of the Earth year, but it was grouped together with the celebration of the winter solstice, the longest night of the year, and became what you now know to be Christmas."

Kimba looked closely at the little figure in the manger. It was amazing that a tiny baby could be the basis for such a big holiday.

"Many families attend special church services during this time," Buddy said. "But we discovered that in other countries, the traditions are very different. Some places, like Japan, love the idea of presents and Santa Claus, but they don't seem to think much about the religious part of the holiday at all. It's a night for romantic dates with a loved one."

"And some countries," Thoth added, motioning to a table table farther down the line, "like in the Czech Republic, focus only on the birth of the baby Jesus and the religious part of the holiday on December twenty-fifth."

The Czech agent at that table nodded to her. "We have celebrations more like your Christmas ones during the night of St. Nicholas, on December fifth. Children may get treats in the streets if they meet the angel walking with St. Nicholas and tell him they were good that year. The devil walks with him too. You don't want a present from him! St. Nicholas, the angel, and the devil may come to your home and read from St. Nicholas's book of who has been good or bad that year. Traditionally, St. Nicholas leaves an orange and some chocolate for good children. Christmas Day itself later in the month is just for going to church and religious celebrations. No tree or presents or anything like that. And you have carp or fish soup for dinner. Come down here and try a sample."

"The soup sounds delicious," Thoth said, "but let's take each table in turn. Next, we have England, where it seems like many of the traditions are the same as in North America. Greetings, Agent Bennett."

"Happy Christmas," Bennett said, his jet-black fur shining in the light of several candles.

"*Happy* Christmas?" Kimba said. "My humans always say *Merry* Christmas."

"I discovered that those phrases come mostly from a very brilliant and honored book called *A Christmas Carol* by an author from England named Charles Dickens. He used the phrase 'Merry Christmas,' and it stuck for many people. However, in England, Queen Elizabeth still says Happy Christmas, so we

173

Brits tend to lean in that direction. One fun tradition in my country is the Christmas cracker."

Bennett motioned to a strange object on his table. It looked like a thin tube of cardboard that was sealed with ribbon on each end, making a sort of hard candy shaped package.

"I'll grab one end, and Kimba, you grab the other. Then we pull and crack it open."

Bennett picked up one end in his teeth, and Kimba hesitantly but obediently picked up the other.

"Pull!" Bennett said around his mouthful.

Both cats leaned back and the cardboard tube ripped open with a loud crack that made Kimba jump. A bit of tissue paper fell out on the floor between them.

"Hey, we got a hat!" Bennett said, dropping his end of the tube.

Kimba spit out her half of the cracker while Bennett shook out the tissue paper and showed her the shape of a crown.

"Oh, Bennett, you are definitely wearing that," Buddy said from the table next to them, shifting his Santa hat with one paw.

Bennett pursed his whiskers but proudly sat the tissue paper crown on his head around both ears.

"Very nice, and very festive," Kimba said. "Happy Christmas, Agent Bennett."

"Happy Christmas, Agent Kimba."

After sampling the carp soup from the Czech Republic and looking at the display on that table, they moved on down the line.

"Greetings, Agent Esperanza," Thoth said to the gray tabby at the next table, who was eagerly awaiting their attention. "Esperanza is one of our agents in the South American portion of Earth."

"You have to hear my speech too," she said with an excited gasp.

"Of course," Kimba said.

"Feliz Navidad!" Esperanza said, adjusting her stance a bit to present her lesson. "That means Merry Christmas or Happy Christmas in Mexico. My last two postings were in small towns in the country of Mexico, and the humans there speak Spanish."

"I've never seen anything like this before," Kimba said, noticing a beautiful plant with massive red leaves displayed on the table.

"This is a poinsettia plant. They grow all over Mexico and are a symbol of the holiday there. Your Earth family has probably never gotten one because they are poisonous if you eat them."

Kimba leaned back a bit from the beautiful red leaves.

"And silly cats tend to try to eat them," Esperanza whispered to her.

"I'm sure it would be tempting," Kimba said. "Those giant leaves look like they would be delicious."

"Delicious, maybe. Deadly, for certain. Don't eat them."

"Okay," Kimba said with a slow-blink.

"But you should try these buñuelos. They are scrumptious. I have some turrón too, but I don't recommend it for cats. It sticks in the teeth."

The buñuelos looked rather like the donut holes Mama sometimes served for breakfast on the weekends.

"Is this what your Earth family in Mexico has for a holiday meal?" Kimba asked.

"It is one of many things," Esperanza said, "but my family doesn't just have one big meal. The parties and celebrations go on for days and days in December. There are parades in the streets. It's amazing."

Kimba resisted the temptation to bat at the giant red flowers in front of her and focused on Esperanza instead.

"The day for presents in Mexico is actually January sixth, El Día de Reyes or Three Kings' Day. See these three figures here?" Esperanza tapped her paw on top of three tall figures in her Nativity scene. "The story tells of three kings who followed a star to find something amazing, and what they found was the baby Jesus. They brought him gifts of gold, frankincense, and myrrh. Children in Mexico also get gifts on this day to celebrate the end of the holiday season."

"What are frankincense and myrrh?" Kimba asked.

"They are saps from trees and plants that are burned to make perfume. It's all very religious and symbolic. But Mexican children get toys and things like that, not smelly tree goo."

177

"Well, that's good," Kimba said, trying to imagine how Mindy and Leia would feel about getting frankincense and myrrh for Christmas.

"And they eat a king cake, like this one." She pointed to a large ring of bread on the table, decorated with bits of red and green fruit. "There's a tiny baby Jesus toy hidden somewhere inside," she whispered to Kimba. "I hope I find it when we start the party."

"A cake with a baby Jesus inside? That is certainly different."

"I also learned from Miss Fluffernutter's research that December celebrations in South America go all the way back to the Aztec and Maya and other groups of humans who lived there thousands of years ago. December has been a party month in South America for almost as long as we cats have been exploring Earth."

"That is a very, very long time," Kimba said.

"It is! But let me tell you, my families in Mexico loved a good long party, usually lasting all night. But we are one of the countries that take Christmas Day itself very seriously. It is a deeply religious and

178

holy holiday in Mexico. Besides church services, they celebrate a little with Las Posadas, where a couple go from house to house asking for a place to stay, like Mary and Joseph in the Bible story. The people in the house sing to them that there is no room and send them away. It's really funny when they try to have the woman playing Mary ride on a donkey. Those animals do not cooperate at all. But it's all in good fun, with lots of food and drink."

Esperanza leaned in closer and whispered, "And it can be a bit extra fun to watch if the humans have had *quite a lot* to drink, if you know what I mean."

Kimba did not know what she meant, but she slow-blinked in return of what she was pretty sure was supposed to be a joke.

"Baby Jesus and his mother, Mary, are important parts of the Mexican culture year round," Esperanza continued. "Many families have statues representing Jesus and Mary that stay on the shelves and tables of the house every day of the year, not just at Christmas."

"Very interesting," Kimba said. "It's amazing how different one holiday can be, depending where on Earth you live."

Thoth nodded his agreement.

"When we started this project," Thoth said, "we had no idea how complicated and involved it would get."

Kimba glanced down the room at the dozen or so tables she had yet to visit, each with an eager agent waiting to share what they had learned about Christmas in their country.

"I can see that," she said. "Very complicated."

For the next thirty minutes, Kimba worked her way around the room and listened carefully. It started to blur together a bit, but she knew they had all worked very diligently and wanted to honor that and be respectful of the work done by each agent.

One of the more interesting tables was an agent from Australia, who displayed a barbeque grill and beach items. In Australia, where the seasons are the opposite of North America, Christmas happens in the summertime, when families are on vacation from school. Children might be camping outdoors at Christmastime. Parties were often more like summer events that Kimba was used to, though they still put up trees and wreaths and all the traditional decorations. It was fascinating.

The few times she glanced over at the high commander, she thought her mother looked pleased.

Partway through, Thoth leaned in close to her and whispered, "Don't worry. There really will be a party and fun and games and a chance to eat the food. It just helped to justify the whole thing if we learned something about Earth along the way. You know how the high commander can be."

Kimba sighed. *Thank goodness!* All of the treats looked too delicious to just talk about.

Feline Nativity Set

19
CLIMBING RACE

Once Kimba had listened to what each agent had to share, the party really began. There were platters of food, and traditional festive music floated through the air from speakers somewhere in the Great Hall. Other cats from the ship wandered in, sampling the food and checking out the displays. Kimba wondered if non-agent cats were interested in Earth culture, or if they just wanted to enjoy the party.

After she had tried food from several different tables, Kimba noticed the cats were all gathering toward the center of the room. When she saw her parents trot in that direction as well, she decided something interesting must be going on and joined the group.

Commander Griffin sauntered through the crowd to the center of the room and stood between two massive pine trees that towered over the crowd. Each was three times as tall as the ceiling of her Earth home, and instead of being on a delicate tree stand like the others around the room, these two still had their roots attached and were set in giant wooden tubs. Both trees were decorated with sparkling ornaments from top to bottom.

"Every party in a room full of agents needs to have a bit of a competition," Griffin said. "So we set up this Christmas tree climbing challenge."

Kimba felt her ears and nose flush bright pink. *How many of these agents know about my grizzly bear encounter in the wilderness room?* she wondered.

Griffin continued, "All of you who have accomplished Earth missions agree that climbing the Christmas tree was strictly forbidden."

The agents nodded to each other in agreement.

"Well, not today!" Griffin announced.

The agents all cheered and yowled.

"And not only will this be a race to climb to the top, you cannot knock off a single dangling, fragile ornament."

Kimba looked the trees up and down. From what she now knew about climbing them, that would be a very tricky task.

"Ten seconds will be added to your time for every ornament you knock off," Griffin said. "Who thinks they can get to the top fastest?"

Amid jeers and thrashing tails, a small group of agents headed for the trees to take their shot. Kimba held back. She had learned to climb a tree, but she knew better than to race those experienced agents to the top.

It was only a few moments before an anxious agent sat at the bottom of each tree, ready to race. They exchanged challenging looks through slanted eyes, and their tails whipped from side to side.

"Ready. Set. Go!" Griffin called out.

185

The pair of agents jumped onto the root ball and then launched themselves into the trees.

Kimba watched in fascination. She couldn't actually see the cats as they climbed because they were hidden among the pine needles, but she could tell where each was along the way by the shifting and twitching of the fir tree as they climbed and balanced on the thin, flexible branches. It reminded her of how the grizzly bear had crashed through the tree limbs, trying to reach her, and she shuddered.

An ornament fell to the floor with a crash, and all the agents cheered.

Before long, a black cat face appeared at the top of one of the trees.

"Victory!" the agent yowled.

"Not so fast!" Griffin called up to him. "You knocked off an ornament. The timer has started for your ten-second penalty."

The suddenly not-victorious agent hissed his frustration, and everyone waited while the clock ticked and the other agent climbed as quickly and as carefully as he could. Branches twitched, getting closer and closer to the top. Griffin leaned over to monitor the stopwatch.

"Time!" yelled the agent in charge of the penalty delay.

"Winner!" Griffin said, pointing to the agent who had been not-so-patiently waiting.

"Waaaoooaaaooo!" the agent howled.

A second later, the other climber popped his head out of the top of his tree and sighed when he realized he was too late.

As the crowd waited for the first two climbers to work their way down, leaving all of the ornaments intact, trays of food were loaded up again.

"This king cake is really good," Kimba said. "It tastes like the bread Mama sometimes shares with me from her meals, but it's even better."

A few more cats tried their skills at the climbing game, and winners were declared. Then some of the winners challenged each other to test who was the very fastest. Kimba had wandered off to look at the displays on some of the tables again when she heard raucous cheers and howls coming from the area around the trees. As she turned to see what it was all about, Thoth raced toward her.

"Come quick," he gasped with pupils so dilated his eyes looked black.

"What's happened? Did someone fall?"

"Oh no, nothing like that. Commander Griffin and your mother are going to race!"

Kimba couldn't imagine her proper and dignified mother climbing a tree in a race, but she followed Thoth back to the pines. The agents parted so she could pass through to the front of the crowd, and there were her parents, sharpening their claws and stretching.

"Griffin is bound to take her," an agent nearby whispered. "When's the last time High Commander Felicity scaled a tree?"

"When's the last time Commander Griffin climbed one?" another agent said in response.

A hush fell over the crowd as the two highest-ranking cats in the known universes stepped up to the base of the trees. Special Agent Artemis moved out of the crowd and took over the judging position.

"First to the top wins," Artemis said. "Don't let any ornaments fall or the same time penalties will apply."

Felicity and Griffin nodded to him. Kimba caught her mother's eyes as she turned back around and was surprised by the excitement twinkling there. The high commander might come across as proper, but she was clearly prepared for this physical challenge.

"Three, two, one, climb!" Artemis called out.

With a leap, both of her parents were up in their trees and quickly out of sight.

Kimba felt the fur rise all over her body, and her tail lashed. The branches shifted on one tree, then the other. Trying to keep track of each parent was difficult, but it seemed like they were staying neck and neck.

The crowd behind her was cheering and howling and calling out encouragement to both competitors, but everyone caught their breath in silence as a limb dipped on Griffin's tree and an ornament seemed to hop right off and land with a *plink*. Then cheers went up again, calling for both of them to climb faster.

189

If Mother can stay even with him, she'll win be-cause of the time penalty, Kimba thought.

She glanced over at Thoth, but his gaze was glued to the tops of the trees, where the branches bobbed up and down with the climbers' movements.

Just as it seemed like one of the cats must pop out of the top at any moment, the branches of Felicity's tree made a wild waggle, and an ornament wiggled loose. It tumbled through the air and landed with a crash, shattering into a thousand pieces.

The crowd went wild. Knowing it was even again, the cheering in the room became deafening. Kimba yowled along with the other agents, not caring a single bit who actually won.

When it felt like the suspense would make her pass out, Kimba saw the calico head of the high commander burst out of the top of the tree. The crowd silenced and looked at Griffin's tree. After only a few seconds more of tussling branches, the black-and-white face of her father poked out of the top.

The agents cheered for both cats, but Artemis declared that High Commander Felicity was the

190

winner. Felicity and Griffin both climbed to the very tip-tops of their trees and sat up tall and proud, each looking like a special feline angel on the Christmas tree. Griffin bowed his head to his mate, and Felicity gave him a satisfied nod in return.

Kimba could see that both of them were puffy, covered in pine needles, and breathing heavily. There was no fix here. They had been genuinely racing.

The crowd settled down, and Felicity and Griffin disappeared back into the branches to start their slow climb back down.

"Aw, he probably let her win," an agent whispered as they walked past Kimba.

"Not a chance," his friend said. "She's not *High Commander* Felicity just because she was born into the right family."

Kimba's heart swelled with pride. She had considered the same thing herself, but she was glad to know it had been a fair race, not just for show.

It also gave her something to consider. Being part of the "right" family didn't mean she wasn't going to have to work hard and prove herself, like her mother—even after Felicity had been in charge for over two hundred years.

Being an Earth cat was much less demanding.

The agents had wandered off and were leaving the party by the time her parents were back on the ground, and Thoth had rushed off to give the transfer technicians directions about returning the trees and decorations to the correct Earth homes.

"Well run, Felicity," Griffin said.

"Thank you," Felicity said with a slow-blink. "I thought I had you for sure when I saw your ornament drop, but all that lead time vanished at the last second when one of mine fell as well. Very exciting!"

Thoth rejoined Kimba and her parents and sat down with a tired plop.

"It's getting close to dawn on Earth," he said. "We don't want any human children to wake up and find their tree gone."

"Goodness no," Griffin said. "Zip it all right back where it belongs."

No sooner had he said that when a tree at the back of the room vanished in a flash of light.

"I guess you don't have to warn trees," Kimba said. "You just transfer them where you want them."

The very last of the agents left the Great Hall, and other cats quickly moved out the tables, treats, and displays from the party. One by one, Christmas trees around them vanished until nothing was left in the Great Hall but the two large trees and the four of them.

"I asked them to wait on these two," Thoth said. "They will need to be stripped of ornaments and replanted in the wilderness room."

"My Daughter," Felicity said, "would you like to try your paws at climbing again?"

Kimba looked up and down the tree trunk. It might not have been taller than the tree she had climbed earlier, but it seemed that way standing in the blank space of the Great Hall.

"Do I have to race?" she asked.

"Of course not," Griffin said. "Thoth, maybe you can join her and make a lesson out of it. I'm sure Agent Janus was not as thorough as you will be."

"Certainly, Commander," Thoth said.

193

He nodded at Kimba, and they both walked over to the trunk of the same tree.

"Since you know what to do for the basics," Thoth said, "I'll follow along behind, in case you need advice."

"Don't you want to get to the top?" she asked. "I doubt I'll make it all that way."

"Getting to the top is not the important part," he said with a twitch of his whiskers.

"What's the important part?"

Thoth pondered his answer for a moment.

"Spending time with a friend is more important than winning a race," he finally said. "Sharpen your claws, and let's go."

While her parents groomed pine needles and sap from their fur, Kimba and Thoth climbed and climbed and knocked ornaments to the ground.

Sometimes on purpose.

20

I'LL BE HOME FOR CHRISTMAS

When Kimba awoke in her new private quarters on her massive fluffy purple pillow, she sighed and stretched. Her muscles objected. Climbing was something they were definitely not used to, but it had been worth it. With Thoth's encouragement and advice, she had finished the climb and looked out over the Great Hall from the top of the Christmas tree. It was one of the proudest moments of her life, one more achievement toward earning her place in the High Command.

But Christmas was over now. The agent observing her human family said they were packing their bags in Michigan and preparing to head back to Arkansas. It was time for Kimba to return to Earth. She groomed a stray pine needle or two from her fur and pressed the red button to let Francis know she was awake. He responded quickly and said he would pick her up for a meal before she departed.

With Francis leading the way, Kimba trotted through the bright-white hallways of the ship to the dining hall. They joined Thoth and the high commander on large pillows and nibbled bits of fish and mouse. It all seemed quite boring after her adventures on the ship over the last few days.

"Are you ready to transfer back home today?" Thoth asked her between bites.

"I suppose so," she said. "It's such a different life here. On Earth, not much ever happens. I watch birds out the window. I sleep and eat. The days blur together."

"That's why agents like your mentor, Special Agent Medusa Gloriosa, choose to retire on Earth. It can be a very uneventful and quiet life."

"Unless you live on the streets," Felicity added. "It's a rare agent who wants to do that."

Living as a stray cat on the streets of Earth did not sound appealing to Kimba at all. She much preferred sleeping in her soft bed high up on Mama's bookshelf with all the stuffed toys.

"We can go to headquarters from here," Thoth said. "They know you're coming and are ready for you." *And if I take you there myself, I can oversee the transfer.*

"Perfect," Felicity said. "I have a meeting with the High Council. Thoth and Francis will see you safely on your way back to Earth."

She rose with a stretch and gave the top of Kimba's head a quick lick.

"Goodbye for now, My Daughter."

Kimba felt a purr rumble up from her throat.

"Goodbye for now, Mother."

Headquarters seemed quieter than usual as Thoth and Kimba trotted toward the transfer platform.

Maybe everyone is tired out from the party, Kimba thought.

But then a loud yowl echoed through the room. They stopped at the unusual sound and looked around. Thoth made a funny coughing noise, and Kimba looked in the same direction. Special Agent Artemis was at his station, and next to him sat Demeter—Slinky and Miss Fatty Cat's mother. Artemis looked over at Thoth and Kimba, and his tail thrashed back and forth.

"Oh, my darling baby!" Demeter wailed. "You must come home soon! How can you survive in that tiny apartment? And with a beast, of all things. How could your girl get a beast when you say you are so important to her?"

"Mother, everything is fine," Slinky's voice came from the computer.

Kimba could just make out Slinky's face on half of the screen as she chatted with her mother from her Earth apartment. Miss Fatty Cat's face showed on the other half of the screen.

198

"No!" Demeter howled again and threw herself down on the keyboard. "It will never be fine until you are home! Why do you make me suffer like this? Don't you love your mother?"

"There, there, Demeter," Artemis said. He gave the black cat a pat or two on the back. "Your daughter is safe and doing her duty as an agent."

Demeter howled and would not be comforted.

"Poor Artemis," Thoth mumbled.

Kimba nodded in agreement. "Poor Slinky."

She sometimes thought Mama was too kissy and huggy, but at least Mama never made a fuss like that.

The pair moved on to the transfer platform and left Artemis to his drama-management duties. Without comment, Kimba climbed up the steps to the transfer platform and sat down. She took several deep, calming breaths while Thoth settled himself at a station and typed in coordinates.

"We are returning you to the same spot we collected you from, right outside the bathroom," Thoth said.

"That's perfect," Kimba said. "The family isn't home yet anyhow, so it really doesn't matter."

"Are you ready, Kimba?"

"Yes," she said. "I'm ready."

"Well then, goodbye until next time."

"See ya later, Thoth," Kimba said with a wink.

Thoth winked back and engaged the system. Kimba felt the tingling in her toes. Then there was a flash of light.

Ten . . . nine . . . eight . . .

The transfer back to Earth was simple, and Kimba felt the cool wood floor of Mama and Daddy's bedroom under her toes before she had counted to five. She saw Hiro asleep on her pillow on top of the cedar chest and wondered if she knew that Daddy would be home shortly.

Instead of waking her sister, Kimba hopped up on the counter. Thoth's face appeared in the mirror. She knew he would still be watching until he was positive she was home safely.

"In case I forgot to say it," she said, "thanks for making my visit to the ship so special and bringing me Christmas in outer space."

"It was my pleasure, Kimba," Thoth said with a twitch of his whiskers.

"It's strange to be back in my quiet house where nobody thinks I'm particularly special."

"The human female seems to appreciate you very much."

"Yes," Kimba admitted. "I suppose she does."

"A Cat in the Mirror will always be watching, if you need anything."

"Thank you, Thoth. It's good to know I can reach you any time I need to."

"I will always be here for you, Kimba."

And he meant it more than she could possibly imagine.

Kimba woke to the sound of the back door opening and the scrabbling of canine toenails on the tile floor of the mud room. The Beast's raspy barks rang through the house as the family clamored inside.

He has lost his voice again, Kimba thought. *Silly Beast.*

Kimba stretched out on Mama and Daddy's bed

and looked over at Hiro. The tuxedo cat was already sitting up tall, eagerly waiting for Daddy to come find her. Kimba knew she wouldn't have to wait long.

Leia screeched by the bedroom door with squeals of joy for Miss Fatty Cat. The fat cat gave a startled squawk in return. Kimba could imagine the massive I-missed-you squeeze Leia had given her.

Daddy was next, coming into the bedroom in search of his Hiro before he even took off his coat.

"There she is," he said with a sigh and hurried around the bed to give Hiro a hug.

Hiro purred and chortled and arched her back to hug him in return.

From all the clunking and banging in the mud room, Kimba guessed that Mama was opening the bags and starting to do laundry right then and there. She remembered the amazing smells of the dirty clothes and towels after the family's visit to Florida a while back. Maybe the laundry was worth checking out.

The white cat hopped down from the bed, trotted past The Big Black Beast—who was doing his usual return-snuffling around the whole house—and into the mud room. She was greeted by open going-away bags and mounds of clothes. Mama stopped with an armload of jeans and smiled at her.

"Well, hello there, Kimba Baby. I see you survived without us." She bent down and extended one finger to bop Kimba on the nose and then scratch under her chin. "One green eye, and one blue eye, just as it should be. Did you have a nice quiet break while we were gone?"

Hardly! Kimba thought. *Not quiet, and certainly not a break.*

"I have a present for you," Mama said.

Kimba hopped into the closest suitcase and sniffed through the contents, wondering what in that mess could possibly be for her. But instead of going there, Mama opened a cabinet in the laundry room and pulled out a small gift bag.

"I should probably wait until later, but who knows where you will be by then. Here. I even wrapped it for you. I know you love to unwrap presents."

Mama set the package on the floor next to the going-away bags, and Kimba jumped out to get it.

After several hesitant sniffs, she grabbed the tissue and pulled it out of the bag. Ripping and shredding it with her back claws, Kimba thought Mama had given her a lovely gift. Mama laughed.

"Silly girl," she said. "There's more in there than just tissue to destroy."

Mama tipped the little bag and out slid a small stuffed toy, the perfect size for Kimba to carry around the house.

"See?" Mama said. "A Christmas present just for you."

Kimba sat and stared at the gift. She couldn't believe her eyes.

"It's a teddy bear of your very own," Mama said. "Now you don't have to steal mine all the time, though maybe the stealing is half the fun."

Kimba sniffed at the toy. *A grizzly bear, of all things.*

Mama couldn't possibly know how perfect a little stuffed bear was after the adventures of the last week. With glee, Kimba grabbed the bear in her teeth and trotted to the sofa with it, singing the whole way.

After the sun went down, the family gathered in the living room. Daddy made a fire in the wood stove while Leia clutched Miss Fatty Cat on the sofa nearby. Mama turned on the colorful spinning Christmas tree topper, and it scattered yellow and red and green flecks of light all around the room. Hiro hopped on the back of the sofa near Daddy's spot, and Kimba curled up with her new toy bear at the other end, where Mama soon joined her. They all sat quietly for a bit, watching the lights and enjoying the tree.

"The decorations at your sister's house were beautiful," Mama said, "but there's something about our own tree in our own house that is extra special."

Kimba slow-blinked at the lights flickering around the room and had to agree. Her Christmas party on the ship had been excellent, and Thoth had outdone himself with the amazing decorations and food, but it still didn't hold a candle to being at home with her family.

"Are you going to be Santa this year?" Leia asked Daddy.

"But of course," he said.

Kimba was confused, but then Daddy grabbed the Santa hat from the back of the sofa and wiggled it down onto his head. Leia giggled. Squatting down in front of the tree, Daddy picked up one of the wrapped presents underneath. Kimba realized there must have been gifts hidden somewhere in the house that were snuck under the tree when the family got home.

"Ho, Ho, Ho!" he said with a laugh. "This one is for Leia."

Leia carefully tore into the package, one tiny rip at a time, trying to guess what it was the whole way through. When she got down to the last bit, she smiled.

"Are those the right ones?" Mama asked.

"These are perfect," Leia said. "My art teacher said these are the best fine-tip markers for my project. Thanks, Mama and Daddy."

While Leia opened the box to check out each

marker color, Daddy continued handing around a few more gifts they had gotten for each other. Mama received a small stuffed white tiger toy to add to her collection. Kimba leaned toward it for a sniff, but Mama set it down out of reach.

"Let the poor tiger have peace for one day," Mama said with a laugh. "You can maul your bear instead."

Fine, Kimba thought. *But one day only.*

When the gifts were done, Daddy brought down the stockings from the mantle. Leia's had some chocolate treats inside. Each of the cats had little bags of their favorite crunchy snacks in their stockings. The Big Black Beast had a bone shaped like a candy cane. He dragged it over to his special pillow and started to gnaw on it immediately.

Finally, everyone settled back on the sofas again. Mama had made some of the warm fruity punch called wassail she always served at Christmas, and each of the humans sipped on a mug of it.

"It's going to be hard to get back to real life after such a lovely vacation," Mama murmured.

"Most definitely," Daddy said with a sigh.

Kimba totally agreed. Daily life was very different from the thrills of that holiday.

"But this is what it's really about," Mama said. "It's not even about a specific day on the calendar. Christmas is about quiet moments like this with the people you love. It's about the spirit of giving, not piles of gifts. All the parties are fun, but the true spirit of Christmas is peace and joy and love. Sometimes it's easier to feel that without a party at all."

Daddy nodded his agreement.

Kimba thought about the thrill of climbing the big fir tree and learning about how Christmas was celebrated around the world, and she had to agree too. Parties were fun, but even better was the calmness of the lights from the tree and the sparks of warmth from the fire and her family gathered together. It was better than a pile of catnip.

"Merry Christmas," Mama said, holding out her mug to Daddy.

"Merry Christmas," Daddy said, gently clinking his mug against hers.

"Merry Christmas," Leia said, holding up her

mug in a pretend clink with each of theirs. She had no intention of getting up and disturbing the cat sleeping in her lap.

"And Merry Christmas, Kimba," Mama said, giving the white cat a gentle stroke on the top of her head.

Merry Christmas, Mama.

Best. Christmas. Ever.

THE END

Silent Night

Silent night, holy night.
All is calm, all is bright
Round yon virgin mother and child.
Holy infant so tender and mild.
Sleep in heavenly peace.
Sleep in heavenly peace.

Silent night, holy night.
Shepherds quake at the sight.
Glories stream from heaven afar.
Heavenly hosts sing Alleluia!
Christ the Saviour is born.
Christ the Saviour is born.

Silent night, holy night.
Son of God, love's pure light.
Radiant beams from thy holy face
With the dawn of redeeming grace,
Jesus, Lord, at thy birth.
Jesus, Lord, at thy birth.

Wassail

64 ounces warm tea

64 ounces real cranberry juice (not cocktail)

64 ounces apple juice

4 cups orange juice, no pulp

6 cinnamon sticks

12 whole cloves

2 cup sugar

1 orange and 1 lemon, sliced

Combine all ingredients in a large pot and bring to a boil. Simmer for 30 minutes and serve. Remove fruit slices, cinnamon sticks, and cloves when saving leftovers.

*For adults, wine or stronger alcohol is often added after the drink is prepared.

If you enjoyed this series, keep reading for a sample chapter of *Bianca: The Brave Frail and Delicate Princess*.

**Best Juvenile Book 2018
Oklahoma Writers' Federation**

Chapter 1

Flames leapt from the dragon's golden jaws and blazed through the sky above the forest.

Princess Bianca didn't flinch. Her tiny feet slipped around inside the stolen boots, but she planted them firmly on the mossy ground and stared straight up past the bronze, armored belly of the beast that threatened her kingdom and every living being for miles around.

As the last flames blew away on the breeze, the dragon glared down at her. Smoke billowed from his nostrils with every breath. People usually ran in fear at the very sight of him, but this girl in ill-fitting peasant clothes stood her ground and planted her hands on her hips.

"Where is my father?" she demanded. "Where is the king? Where are the knights who rode with him?"

The dragon bent his mammoth head down until he hovered only inches above her. Tendrils of smoke swirled around her dark, curly hair as he chortled with amusement.

"I would imagine the same thing happened to them as has befallen every other knight and king who rides against me."

He poofed a quick flame above her head as an example and tipped his face so they were now eye to eye.

"Then you are going to be one sorry dragon."

One Month Earlier

Princess Bianca had never been so bored in all thirteen years of her cushy, royal existence. And that was saying something. Most of the days of her life in the Kingdom of Pacifico blended together and rambled on and on with a sameness that could numb the sharpest spirit. But now that she was getting too old for tutors, there were not even those dull lessons to look forward to.

Princess Bianca knew she shouldn't complain. She had everything in the world she would ever possibly need. Her father, King Dominic, loved her to the point of smothering. And she was told daily that everyone in the kingdom thought she was the most wonderful princess who had ever lived.

Every afternoon, at precisely one o'clock, she would wave to her subjects from a window up high in her castle tower, and they would cheer and wave back.

"She is so beautiful and dainty," the men would say. "We are so lucky to have such a perfect example of princessness in our kingdom."

"Never a hair out of place," the women would say with a sigh. "Constantly smiling and so gracious."

Bianca's bedroom was always full of flowers that were left on the castle steps by children—and sometimes even by bold young men, who hoped to gain her attention in a different way altogether. The boys, however, were wasting their time. Nanny and the multitude of servants who dealt with bringing the flowers to Bianca's room never mentioned a single name. Cards bearing declarations of love were burned on the kitchen hearth.

"Stupid boys," Nanny would snipe. "Nothing better to do with their time and energy than pile flowers on our delicate princess, who will never choose her own husband anyhow."

Cook would nod and agree.

Princess Bianca could be admired from afar, but not one of those young men would ever get within one hundred feet of her.

"Their parents should have better control of them and get them out in the fields for some useful work," Cook would say as she stirred whatever pot of deliciousness she had created for the next royal meal.

Standing above the daily fray of flowers and adoration, the princess was grateful that the townspeople loved her. She knew not every kingdom had loyal subjects. But what would really bring her joy was to throw open the castle doors, frolic through the green grass, and kick up dirt on the dusty paths with those same children who flocked to her window every afternoon.

However, that was not allowed.

Not ever.

From the time the princess was born, everyone had said that she was so frail and so delicate that she must be protected diligently. Her mother, Queen Ariana the Kind, had not survived the birth, and Bianca had nearly joined her in the grave. For weeks, the nurses had stayed by her side every moment and documented each cough and sneeze. Then those weeks extended into months . . . and into years.

King Dominic was terrified that he would lose his beloved daughter to illness or her own frailty, so he kept her hidden away inside the strong castle walls. The doctor had stressed how weak she was at birth, and the king would not take any chances. Of course, that was thirteen years ago, but her father never overcame his fears or his safeguarding of each second of her life.

Never, not for an instant, was she allowed to meet other children. Playing with one was out of the question. Who knew what kinds of diseases they carried?

Never, not for even one brief moment, had she been allowed outside the castle fortifications. The gray stone walls of the enormous fortress had been built by her ancestors over many centuries. It was like a city unto itself, designed for safety and protection from attack. For Bianca, the castle had become a shield from the outside world—and a prison she couldn't escape.

Princess Bianca could dream of what grass felt like, but she had never touched it. Not once. She could wander around within the castle walls to the stable and such, but there was nothing there but hard-packed dirt paths. The daily flowers in her room were the only bit of nature she was allowed. That tradition of bringing her flowers had started with her dangerous birth as gifts and well-wishes from the kingdom, and her father had allowed it to continue.

Carefully selected tutors had been brought into the castle to teach her to read, do math, learn to speak five useless languages for countries she would never visit, play the piano, create elaborate needlework, and ensure that she was the most accomplished young lady in the kingdom. And she certainly was because most girls didn't have eight hours a day to devote to such tasks.

The king was delighted and proud.

But the princess was lonely and bored.

No matter what was said about her, the princess did not *feel* frail or delicate. She had heard the stories of her birth and the doctor's warnings—over and over and over—but none of it seemed a part of her own lungs and heart and arms and legs. It was as if they were fussing about a stranger she had never met. Many times she had tried to get her father to let her venture outside the castle. Maybe just for a walk or to ride a horse quietly through the woods, surrounded by soldiers.

"But what if you fall off?" the king would wail. "What if there is an angry bumblebee or a rain storm or a cold wind, or what if . . . ?"

Her father always had a "what-if" for any plea she made. Eventually, the princess had just given up, resigned to the fact that her life would be dull and sheltered and protected forever.

But when no one was looking, she would sneak away and race through the quiet hallways of the castle. She would pull off her fancy shoes, hike up her frilly dress, and take the stairs two at a time. And there were thousands of stairs. She would sneak the swords off the displays of suits of armor and pretend to fight invading forces and murderous monsters. Imaginary warriors and mighty dragons would drop in her path as she wielded the sword bravely through the hallways and up and down the staircases.

Of course, she always won.

Then she would fix her hair, straighten her dress, put her dainty shoes back on, and return to Nanny and her maids as though nothing had ever happened.

But that day, the day she was the most bored she had ever been in her entire sheltered existence, there appeared to be no escape from her tedious captivity. The castle was full of people, so nowhere would be truly safe for running and playing. And Nanny surely wouldn't let her get near that many citizens anyhow. Coming into contact with a person from outside the castle was avoided at all costs for the Frail and Delicate Princess Bianca. Nanny would have her guard up and probably even skip her afternoon nap just to keep an eye on the princess.

To make matters worse, it was raining for the third day in a row, and no one even showed up to greet her at one o'clock because the mud was so deep.

Looking out over the murky courtyard on that rainy day, that was the most depressed that Bianca had ever been. The smiling faces of her townspeople were one of the few bright spots in her mundane life, but that day she was deprived of them as well. She flopped down on her very pink fluffy bed in her very pink frilly room and sighed.

Since the castle was too busy for her to sneak off and fight imaginary monsters, she pulled a book of fairy tales from her bedside table and propped herself up to read her favorites . . . again. Books were another bright spot she could always count on. She could lose herself there in all the adventures she would never have. If only her own kingdom could be so exciting and full of magic, like fairies and dragons and witches.

And so that was how Bianca expected her life to continue.

Day after day.

Year after year.

But an unexpected and unwelcome visitor to her kingdom would upend it all.

Unknown to Princess Bianca, there was a dark reason all the townspeople had come to the castle that day. For weeks, horrible news had spread like a thick winter fog from the outlying farms to the villages and to the king himself.

At first, the king brushed it off as only a rumor, but now there were too many frightened citizens to ignore. He was forced to face the fact that the terrible stories of impending devastation and ruin must be true. The invader even the strongest and bravest king feared with his whole being was heading their way.

It would prove without a doubt that Bianca's kingdom was more magical than she had been led to believe.

End of Chapter 1 Sample

Don't Miss Meg's Other Books
Some Dog-Gone Good Adventures

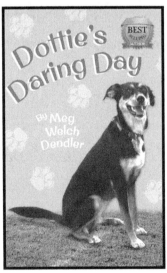

And For Older Readers

Penny had been stuck in the same cozy diner for decades—ever since she died in 1952. Then ridiculously handsome bad boy biker Jake dropped in and became stuck as well, turning her world upside down. Should Penny risk losing it all for a chance at love?

Being part tiger and part human should be an advantage—not lead to extermination. Young tigran Taliya has been forced to flee her home. Paired with a male white tigran named Kano, Taliya is determined to survive, but what awaits her is more challenging than she ever imagined.

If you enjoyed Kimba's story, please take a moment to leave a review at Amazon.com or Goodreads.com and tell your friends!

Sign up for Meg's Reader's Group (at megdendler.com) to hear about new books, sales, and other exciting events in the lives of Kimba and her friends.

AUTHOR'S NOTE

It felt like the series could not be complete without a Christmas story, and I hope you enjoyed reading about Kimba's holiday adventures.

Christmas is a special time of year for many families around the world, and it is a favorite holiday in our home. All of our cats loved hanging out under the tree or running off with an ornament on occasion. They did try to climb the plastic tree when they were kittens, but they gave that up quickly.

227

Miss Fatty Cat looks like she's blocking the river in the Christmas village.

Hiro, under the tree and in the village, carefully not knocking anything down.

What is also true—yucky, but true—is that both Hiro and Kimba liked to use the sink instead of a litter box. They were so tiny when we rescued them, I had to actually help them go potty after they ate. The mama cat usually does this. Oh, the things you learn when you try to raise a tiny creature. I would use a cotton ball to help them go potty while holding them over the sink, in case there were accidents. Our theory is that they associated the smell of the drain with a place to do their business. Lesson learned. As adult cats, they used the litter box roughly 50% of the time, maybe more for Kimba. I cleaned sinks a lot.

Agent Janus is a returning character, and he is based on several cats I have seen on the internet. Doing some research, I discovered that two-faced cats like him are actually often something very unique. He is a "chimera cat," and there is a biological explanation for his two colors. It happens when two embryos merge or join together inside the mother cat's womb. Instead of one egg splitting, which would result in identical twins, two eggs join and make a new creature that is basically different on each side: half and half. This doesn't just happen to cats either. It can happen to many species, including humans, though it often goes unnoticed because we don't have fur. Very unique!

The name Janus comes from ancient Roman tradition as the god of beginnings, gates, transitions, time, duality, doorways, passages, and endings. He is usually depicted as having two faces—looking to the future and to the past. The Romans didn't necessarily have the negative sense we put on being "two-faced," but that twist on it is definitely my intent: someone who appears to be one thing but is really something completely different, like an undercover spy or a friend who only pretends to like you but says horrible things behind your back.

I've never had a reader comment about the fact that the cats in my books see colors. Maybe they just go with me on the "suspension of disbelief" that is involved in alien cats in the first place. Scientist believe cats see limited colors, if any, but that's not really much fun. My take is that alien cats have simply tricked scientists. They can see all the colors of the rainbow and enjoy them as well.

The tradition of bringing greenery inside during

the winter started long before Christianity and Christmas trees. From Ancient Egypt to Imperial Rome to the Vikings, plants that stayed green all year were used as part of the celebrations of the winter solstice, the longest day of the year. In many countries it was believed that evergreens would keep away witches, ghosts, evil spirits, and illness.

Germany is credited with what we now know as a Christmas tree. It is widely accepted that the Protestant reformer Martin Luther was the first to add lighted candles to a tree. I'm glad we stick with electric strands of lights these days because dozens of candles on a live tree sounds kind of dangerous.

In the 1800s, German settlers brought this tradition to America, though it was still seen as odd if not a bit pagan. In some parts of the country, it was illegal to sing carols or put up decorations or any other activity that was outside of the church. When Queen Victoria was sketched enjoying a Christmas tree in the palace with her large family (her husband, Prince Albert, was German), religious conservatism slowly yielded to being fashionable. By the 1900s, Christmas trees were firmly established as a holiday tradition.

Whatever season of the year finds you reading this book, I hope you have enjoyed it and all of Kimba's alien cat adventures.

Kimba, preparing for a nap under the tree

GRATITUDE

Many thanks go out to Crystal Ursin, Luis Contreras, Kathryn Lane, and Chris Raymond for their help in describing how Christmas is celebrated in genuine Mexican tradition. Several friends, including Alice White, helped me with the British side of things, and my years of working alongside the Pospisil family taught me about Christmas in the Czech Republic. The rest is based on research, so any errors are my own.

A multitude of thanks go to my writing critique group, Ozark Mountain Guild of Writers (OMG), for giving me notes on nearly every page of this story. You can thank comedic writer extraordinaire Russell Gayer for suggesting a litter box training room.

And a big thank you to Laura Matthews at thinkStory.biz for giving the final book one last going-over and proofread. We've both come a long way from our years of working on the Spiritually Significant Cinema columns, and I knew I could count on you with this newest book baby.

And, as always, I'm grateful to my husband and daughters for reading copies of this story and giving me ideas along the way.

Finally, to my readers: THANK YOU!!

WORDS YOU MAY NOT KNOW

The teacher in me loves to throw fun words into my stories, but you may find that some of them are new to you. Here's a few from each chapter, just in case you need to check on what they mean in the story.

Chapter 1

prickery: (adj.) word made up by the author to indicate something very sharp that could prick your skin

carport: (noun) a sideless covered area attached to a building, designed to store a car; like a garage but only a roof without walls

Nativity: (noun) birth, or more specifically in this usage the birth of Jesus and the traditions that revolve around that scene in the barn

trinkets: (noun) small ornaments or items, usually of little monetary value or cost

jockey: (verb) to move cleverly or skillfully

bustled: (verb) moved with a great show of energy or enthusiasm; hustled or hurried

miscommunicated: (verb) communicated or passed on information unclearly, with errors, or mistakenly

conduct: (noun) personal behavior or way of acting

predator: (noun) a hunter or creature that preys on other animals

pupils: (noun) the black centers of the eyes that expand or contract to allow the right amount of light to enter and reach the retinas

canine: (noun) dog

"a different tack": (idiom) to try another approach or way of doing something; term used in boat sailing, where you change tack to quickly alter the direction the boat is going

Chapter 3

embed: (verb) inserted, attached, or made something a part of another thing

regulate: (verb) govern or bring into control; adjust to a standard or requirement

perked: (verb) raised briskly, quickly, or at attention

pouting: (verb) acting sad, moody, or sullen

Chapter 4

contraption: (noun) a gadget, device, or useful item, often complicated in nature and structure

patch: (verb) to connect or hook up; to join in on a radio conversation

Chapter 5

averted: (verb) turned away or off to the side, often to prevent something

distinctive: (adj.) having an uncommon quality; separate or different than normal, often in a positive or good way

"of all the nerve": (idiom) used to express shock and disapproval; to have "nerve" often means to act in a way that others feel is wrong or disapprove of or to be bold and daring

"cool and collected": (idiom) calm and in control of one's behavior; having one's emotions under control or "collected" in one place; poised and dignified

"by gum": (idiom) old-fashioned phrase used to show determination, sometimes considered a mild form of cursing instead of saying "by God"; nothing to do with chewing gum

cadet: (noun) a student in a military academy or similar training program, used here to refer to being a student in agent training on the ship

combat: (adj.) fight or battle, usually in a trained and specific way

dainty: (adj.) delicate and beautiful; small and often fragile

"fit the bill": (idiom) very prepared or perfect for a specific job or responsibility; from the theater, where an actor would be just right for a role

Chapter 6

tufted: (adj.) having a bunch or cluster of soft parts, in this case hairs, attached together closely at the base and farther apart at the ends; having a tuft of hair

pivotal: (adj.) of vital importance; highly important; changing the course of something or causing it to pivot in a new direction

fiasco: (noun) a complete and total failure; disaster

tactfully: (adv.) using good sense of what to say in a given situation without upsetting anyone; being diplomatic and careful about what is said and done, especially in a difficult situation

busybody: (noun) a person who meddles and fusses in the lives of other people and is generally considered a problem and annoyance

exile: (noun) a forced separation from a home or country, often for political reasons; a banishment from home or country

Chapter 7

agitated: (adj.) excited, unsettled, disturbed, or possibly angry

closure: (noun) bringing to an end or closing completely; a sense of mental certainty and completion of an idea

hygiene: (noun) a condition of cleanliness, usually involving bathing and being free of germs, to maintain a healthy bodily condition

diligent: (adj.) ongoing, persistent, and constant effort to accomplish something; painstaking effort toward a goal

Chapter 8

gawk: (verb) to stare stupidly or impolitely; stare at something for longer than is necessary, usually in awe or shock

peach fuzz: (noun) short, soft hairs that feel like the fuzzy skin on a peach

clenched: (verb) squeezed, closed up, or knotted up tightly

ridicule: (noun) speech, action, or laughter that causes the subject to feel embarrassment or shame, often intentional or mocking

Chapter 9

riser: (noun) step or platform that is higher than the ground around it

quadrupled: (verb) made four times as large or four times as great; quad = four

expectantly: (adv.) having expectations or looking for a specific outcome; anticipating or looking forward to something

Chapter 10

precariously: (adv.) dangerously, riskily, and without a sure foundation or outcome

matron: (noun) a woman who supervises or is in charge of children

rally: (verb) to muster or gather together for a common purpose; to call to order

industrious: (adj.) diligent; constantly, regularly busy and occupied with useful work

tidy: (adj.) cleaned up and restored to order

diplomat: (noun) one skilled in conversations and negotiations between countries or governments, in this case an agent or High Council member

ponder: (verb) to think about or consider thoughtfully

Chapter 11

menacing: (adj.) threatening; promising to cause harm or injury

hyper: (adj.) overexcited, wild, or keyed up; short for hyperactive

insistent: (adj.) demanding, persistent, or determined to see a certain outcome

Chapter 12

reluctantly: (adv.) with hesitation or unwillingly; pausing in consideration before acting

anxious: (adj.) greatly worried and filled with anxiety; mentally distressed; upset and fearful

practicality: (noun) usefulness or design for an actual purpose or job; serving a purpose and being of real use

sheaths: (noun) coverings on the claws that are like dead skin and need to be removed from time to time, like a snake sheds its skin

exhilarating: (adj.) cheerful, thrilling, and exciting, but in a positive way

Chapter 13

rouse: (verb) to wake up; bring out of a state of sleepiness or inactivity

volition: (noun) a choice or willing decision

Chapter 14

route: (noun) a way, course, or pathway of travel

"get your bearings": (idiom) to figure out where you are and become comfortable in your situation or surroundings

trepidation: (noun) fear, nervous worry, or fright, often involving trembling and panic

Chapter 15

tentatively: (adv.) hesitantly, unsurely, or carefully

forbidden: (adj.) against the rules, prohibited, something not allowed, or a big no-no

reprimand: (noun) scolding, yelling at, or criticism

urgency: (noun) a state of moving quickly, expressing immediate action and results

Chapter 16

tirade: (noun) a long, drawn-out speech, usually bitter, angry, and forceful

envy: (verb) wanting something someone else has; being jealous

rankled: (verb) caused upset, irritation, or bitterness, like rubbing a cat's fur the wrong way

Chapter 17

festive: (adj.) joyous, merry, and prepared for a festival or holiday event

nestle: (verb) to cuddle or snuggle down, like a bird in a nest

rendition: (noun) a version or interpretation, often of a piece of music or art

enthusiastic: (adj.) excited, engaged, eager, or full of passion

strewn: (verb) scattered, spread widely, or thrown about

Chapter 18

scrumptious: (adj.) something especially delicious

frankincense: (noun) an aromatic gum sap or resin from various trees, used for burning of incense in religious ceremonies and other medicinal uses as well

myrrh: (noun) an aromatic resin from various plants that are tall and spiny, used as incense or as perfume

Aztec: (noun) a civilization of people who lived in Central Mexico around 1300 to 1600 CE, before European explorers arrived

Maya: (noun) a civilization of people who lived in South America from at least 1800 BCE, if not earlier, until 250 CE

Chapter 19

jeers: (noun) taunts, teasing, or sometimes rude yelling

penalty: (noun) a disadvantage given to one side of a competition for breaking a rule or having some offending action during the competition

victorious: (adj.) having earned status as winner, champion, or victor

raucous: (adj.) loud, wild, and maybe even out of control

scaled: (verb) climbed or went up something, like a ladder

fix: (noun) to decide and prearrange an outcome, regardless of the actual abilities of the contestants, as in "to fix a race," usually illegally

Chapter 20

coordinates: (noun) any numbers used to determine a specific point on a line or a map or in space

clamored: (verb) created noisy shouting, a racket, or loud activity

"didn't hold a candle": (idiom) something or someone has so much talent, beauty, or appeal that nothing else can possibly be worth comparing to it

maul: (verb) to handle roughly, attack, or cause harm to with a rough beating

ABOUT THE AUTHOR

Meg Dendler has considered herself a writer since she won a picture book contest in fifth grade and entertained her classmates with ongoing sequels for the rest of the year. Beginning serious work as a freelancer in the 1990s while teaching elementary and middle school, Meg has more than one hundred articles in print, including interviews with Kirk Douglas, Sylvester Stallone, and Dwayne "The Rock" Johnson. She has won contests with her short stories and poetry, along with multiple international awards for her best-selling "Cats in the Mirror" alien rescue cat children's book series. *Bianca: The Brave Frail and Delicate Princess* was named Best Juvenile Book of 2018 by the Oklahoma Writers' Federation.

Meg and her family live in Arkansas.

Visit her at www.megdendler.com for more information about upcoming books and events and all of Meg's social media links.

Made in the USA
Middletown, DE
08 September 2021

47110607R10149